Prairie Schooner
Book Prize in Fiction
EDITOR: Hilda Raz

University of
Nebraska Press
LINCOLN
and LONDON

Bliss

and Other Short Stories

TED GILLEY

Manufactured in the United States of America

Library of Congress Cataloging-in-Publication Data
Gilley, Ted.
Bliss and other short stories / Ted Gilley.
p. cm. — (Prairie schooner book prize in fiction)
ISBN 978-0-8032-3261-7 (pbk. : alk. paper)
1. Happiness—Fiction. I. Title.
PS3607.I4443B65 2010
813'.6—dc22   2009050224

Set in Arno Pro by Kim Essman.
Designed by A. Shahan.

For my mother,
and to the memory
of my father

Contents

Acknowledgments

Some of the stories in this collection
        were previously published:
"Bliss" in *New England Review* 29,
        no. 3 (2008)
"House of Prayer" in *The Other Side*,
        November/December 2003
"The End Zone" in *Prairie Schooner* 75,
        no. 4 (Winter 2001)
"Physical Wisdom" in *Northwest
        Review* 32, no. 2 (1994)
"Mountains of the Moon" in *Northwest
        Review* 30, no. 3 (1992)
"Invisible Waves" in *Northwest Review*
        30, no. 1 (1992)

All Hallows' Eve

Horses are the new children. Pasture and field in high-autumn shades of bruised red and yellow, aroma of horse-apples and hay, sweetness of harvest and rot. White fencing, a kitchen dooryard and the white farmhouse with cellar workshop, passive solar, a royal flush of hardwood floors, a black, white, and chrome kitchen, offices, cedar chests piled deep with quilts against the cold New England winter nights, just commencing. Plantings, views, privacy deck. A pair of pristine barns shaken free of chattels. And two men.

"I'm just saying," Jamie says.

"I *hear* what you're saying." Sirut puts a hand on Jamie's Saab, lifts it off.

"Yeah, thanks, I don't want that to get scratched"—his eye on Sirut's ring.

"I'm hip to that." Sirut's lingo amusing and dated, here and there a phrase of American he might have learned from a soldier. He glances at his own car, a Chevy. It announces his lack of affluence—*I am a very used and very tired car*—and he wishes he could have parked it elsewhere. But where? No practical arrangement for parking is laid out. So, he brought it down into the yard and parked it beside this nice expensive one.

Jamie says, "She'll be back in, I don't know. Fifteen minutes?"

Janie, he means. *Jamie and Janie*. In Sirut's country, the similarity in names would be a love sign, a small domestic marvel, celebrated. Here it is a smirk.

"I mean, I plan to get as much as I paid. Even more—you can get that. Saabs don't decline in value."

There is a swish of gravel from under the trees they both believe is caused by Janie's car. Hers is the last house on the road, the nearest neighbor is half a mile away. *Locals*, Jamie called them. Sirut gazes into the red and yellow foliage roasting in the declining sun. In Cambodia, there were only, finally, *locals*. Millions of *locals*.

Janie's car rolls into the kitchen yard.

"So, you'll stay to dinner?"

Sirut is silent. He would prefer to speak with Janie, and alone—had meant to find her here *alone*. After all, Janie is divorced, she told him so only the day before: Did he understand? *Yes, we have divorce in Cambodia*, he had replied, grinning. (*I'm hip to that.*) He did not say, *The divorce of all from all*. No point.

But to find the former husband here, walking out from the house, a cup of coffee in hand, a big smile on his big face. *You must be Sirut.* Must I!

"I do not understand." Sirut hears Janie's car door snap shut; he is aware of her diminishing distance from them, even though all is quiet here, muffled cleanly—in winter, too, drifts, floods of snow! Nights so cold your bones could crack. And in these woods, what? Isolation. A far-off buzzing of cars or a single-engine plane with its sad, brassy note blurted across the tops of the trees. The cough and catch of a chain saw.

We escaped the city, she said. She and her husband—this Jamie—had wanted a positive lifestyle, horses, a house, careers that could be plugged in, unplugged, transported, updated. And they wanted to see the world. *Before it's too late*, she said, serious all of a sudden.

They'd been drinking gin-and-tonics at the party his American sponsors had given in honor of his birthday. Everyone was a little drunk. He had met Janie half an hour earlier, and he was in love. *In my country*, he said, handing her a fresh, icy drink—and stopped. He had been telling stories about his country all day! What he wanted now was to kiss this woman, to obliterate *country* in a rush toward her: to stake a claim.

"What can I tell you?" Jamie says. He polishes the car with a chamois, then lifts his arms away to view and to display the clouds crowding the black, gleaming surface. "It's an arrangement that works for us. I still live here because, for now, it's convenient. For now. Hey, Janie."

"Hey. Hi, Sirut! What's convenient?" She is wearing an elegant and unfussy, secondhand-store-quality dress. But new. Expensive.

"Snowing down south," Jamie sings.

Janie tugs at the dress's hem. "Sirut, it's so nice to see you."

"Okay, you two." Jamie points at them with six-shooter fingers. "That's my cue. Be good. I'm off to the village."

"Pick up some mums."

"Will do."

"And pumpkins. *Three*, Jamie. Three pumpkins."

The Saab's engine turns over. Janie turns to Sirut. "What was convenient?"

"I do not understand." Sirut keeps his eyes on Jamie's car as it climbs the graded slope of yard and mounts the gravel road beside the house. "I do not understand." The car disappears into the shade beneath the darkening foliage. When night comes, these hills close in like jungle, and in the dark, there's no difference at all.

Pumpkins for their porch—he's seen this already: spooks and witches, ghosts and goblins. Haunted houses. A haunted country, but haunted by what? *I'm hip to that*, the Khmer soldier had said in bad American, putting the barrel of the pistol into Sirut's father's ear and pulling the trigger. Laughing soldiers returning his mother to him, used, mute, her mind and soul scoured clean.

They escaped the city, then the camps, finally the country.

The horses drift over, ears erect: Is something up?

Do unto me, their eyes say.

"I simply do not understand," Sirut says.

The horses stir, then drift back to their grazing. Long necks arc, the big heads' extravagant lips fuss and ruffle the grass.

"Sirut," she says. "Tell me what was convenient before."

Bliss

All my life, I seem to have been mistaken for someone else. The other day, a woman stopped me in the produce aisle at the market and said, "Michael?" When I pick up heart pills for my dad, the pharmacist always says, "Hi, Tim." When I correct him, he smiles and says, "Good to see you." When I walk down Idle Road from my apartment to my job, or along the highway, people I don't know wave at me from cars. I wave back, it can't hurt. One day a girl leaned out of a car as it shot by and yelled, "I love you, Jamie!" I am introduced to people over and over again. "Have we met?" they say. "It's Walter, or Phil, or Daniel, isn't it?" I have wondered if wearing a name tag would be a bad idea. *Hello, I'm Cleave.* Who could forget such a name? When I look in the mirror I realize that I am, to some extent, a fabrication. The face looks like mine, all right, but also looks, vaguely, like anyone's: a racial cameo of smooth skin, fine hair. Mouth, nose, and eyes all where they should be, but somehow indistinct—the anonymous, undeclared face of a baby. A face you could put a face onto, including your own, or that of someone close to you whom you've not seen in you can't remember how long. *"Michael?"* When the lady in the store said that, I just smiled and shook my head—and she looked confused, hurt, angry. Who had she lost? *Yes*, I wanted to say, but didn't. *Yes, it's me.*

I stepped from the mud and rain of my midday duties into the outer sanctum of the Pritchard Publishing Company. It isn't what people think. No one ever says to me, *Oh*—you work for a *publisher*, because everyone around here knows that there is only one such out-

5

fit in this part of the state and that it is owner-operated by the crazy Pritchards, purveyors of four-color brochures to the attractions of the Green Mountains. It's a reprint operation. Mr. Pritchard is our only "author." *Oh,* folks are more likely to say. You work for *them.*

And there is nothing glamorous about what I do: I am the "general help."

When I came in, Mrs. Goodell, our executive secretary, blinked her smartly made-up martyr's eyes at me in a code I could not interpret. She held up her heavily ringed hands; silver bangles rattled into the sleeves of her red blazer. Mr. Pritchard was burning up the telephone in the inner sanctum. "I can't stand this," Mrs. G. said. But I knew that she could. "And Cleave," she added in a register of confidence and woe, "I have to tell you, there are no checks today."

"Excuse me?" I said.

One of my jobs is to take paychecks to Billy and Jill, who make runs to the printer and distribute our materials. They usually hang out at the warehouse on Idle Road, minutes from here but far from here, if you know what I mean. Naturally, it registered that Mrs. G. meant *my* check, too, and I went into meditation mode, or tried to— not easy, what with Jack Pritchard ordering his daughter, LeeAnne, in a voice normally reserved for summoning Satan, to bring him the *receivables,* and she screaming that she could not find them and had he forgotten that receivables were not her *bailiwick*?

Their offices are two doors apart.

Nevertheless, I willed an interior stillness, visualized the cosmos within, and ascended: I looked down on the building, then rose higher, floating over the local greenery, then the county, the state— and on and on in a series of diminishing images until the earth disappeared in the litter of space and I approached the peace and quiet of infinite distance with its cool, clean open-ended light-years.

Someone spoke my name.

I opened my eyes. Mrs. Goodell was looking at me with concern. "Cleave, are you all right?"

"Mrs. G.," I said, "I'm fine. But I do need to be paid."

Contents

Acknowledgments

Some of the stories in this collection
were previously published:
"Bliss" in *New England Review* 29,
no. 3 (2008)
"House of Prayer" in *The Other Side*,
November/December 2003
"The End Zone" in *Prairie Schooner* 75,
no. 4 (Winter 2001)
"Physical Wisdom" in *Northwest
Review* 32, no. 2 (1994)
"Mountains of the Moon" in *Northwest
Review* 30, no. 3 (1992)
"Invisible Waves" in *Northwest Review*
30, no. 1 (1992)

Bliss and Other Short Stories

All Hallows' Eve

Horses are the new children. Pasture and field in high-autumn shades of bruised red and yellow, aroma of horse-apples and hay, sweetness of harvest and rot. White fencing, a kitchen dooryard and the white farmhouse with cellar workshop, passive solar, a royal flush of hardwood floors, a black, white, and chrome kitchen, offices, cedar chests piled deep with quilts against the cold New England winter nights, just commencing. Plantings, views, privacy deck. A pair of pristine barns shaken free of chattels. And two men.

"I'm just saying," Jamie says.

"I *hear* what you're saying." Sirut puts a hand on Jamie's Saab, lifts it off.

"Yeah, thanks, I don't want that to get scratched"—his eye on Sirut's ring.

"I'm hip to that." Sirut's lingo amusing and dated, here and there a phrase of American he might have learned from a soldier. He glances at his own car, a Chevy. It announces his lack of affluence—*I am a very used and very tired car*—and he wishes he could have parked it elsewhere. But where? No practical arrangement for parking is laid out. So, he brought it down into the yard and parked it beside this nice expensive one.

Jamie says, "She'll be back in, I don't know. Fifteen minutes?"

Janie, he means. *Jamie and Janie.* In Sirut's country, the similarity in names would be a love sign, a small domestic marvel, celebrated. Here it is a smirk.

"I mean, I plan to get as much as I paid. Even more—you can get that. Saabs don't decline in value."

There is a swish of gravel from under the trees they both believe is caused by Janie's car. Hers is the last house on the road, the nearest neighbor is half a mile away. *Locals*, Jamie called them. Sirut gazes into the red and yellow foliage roasting in the declining sun. In Cambodia, there were only, finally, *locals*. Millions of *locals*.

Janie's car rolls into the kitchen yard.

"So, you'll stay to dinner?"

Sirut is silent. He would prefer to speak with Janie, and alone—had meant to find her here *alone*. After all, Janie is divorced, she told him so only the day before: Did he understand? *Yes, we have divorce in Cambodia*, he had replied, grinning. (*I'm hip to that.*) He did not say, *The divorce of all from all*. No point.

But to find the former husband here, walking out from the house, a cup of coffee in hand, a big smile on his big face. *You must be Sirut.*

Must I!

"I do not understand." Sirut hears Janie's car door snap shut; he is aware of her diminishing distance from them, even though all is quiet here, muffled cleanly—in winter, too, drifts, floods of snow! Nights so cold your bones could crack. And in these woods, what? Isolation. A far-off buzzing of cars or a single-engine plane with its sad, brassy note blurted across the tops of the trees. The cough and catch of a chain saw.

We escaped the city, she said. She and her husband—this Jamie—had wanted a positive lifestyle, horses, a house, careers that could be plugged in, unplugged, transported, updated. And they wanted to see the world. *Before it's too late*, she said, serious all of a sudden.

They'd been drinking gin-and-tonics at the party his American sponsors had given in honor of his birthday. Everyone was a little drunk. He had met Janie half an hour earlier, and he was in love. *In my country*, he said, handing her a fresh, icy drink—and stopped. He had been telling stories about his country all day! What he wanted now was to kiss this woman, to obliterate *country* in a rush toward her: to stake a claim.

"What can I tell you?" Jamie says. He polishes the car with a chamois, then lifts his arms away to view and to display the clouds crowding the black, gleaming surface. "It's an arrangement that works for us. I still live here because, for now, it's convenient. For now. Hey, Janie."

"Hey. Hi, Sirut! What's convenient?" She is wearing an elegant and unfussy, secondhand-store-quality dress. But new. Expensive.

"Snowing down south," Jamie sings.

Janie tugs at the dress's hem. "Sirut, it's so nice to see you."

"Okay, you two." Jamie points at them with six-shooter fingers. "That's my cue. Be good. I'm off to the village."

"Pick up some mums."

"Will do."

"And pumpkins. *Three*, Jamie. Three pumpkins."

The Saab's engine turns over. Janie turns to Sirut. "What was convenient?"

"I do not understand." Sirut keeps his eyes on Jamie's car as it climbs the graded slope of yard and mounts the gravel road beside the house. "I do not understand." The car disappears into the shade beneath the darkening foliage. When night comes, these hills close in like jungle, and in the dark, there's no difference at all.

Pumpkins for their porch—he's seen this already: spooks and witches, ghosts and goblins. Haunted houses. A haunted country, but haunted by what? *I'm hip to that*, the Khmer soldier had said in bad American, putting the barrel of the pistol into Sirut's father's ear and pulling the trigger. Laughing soldiers returning his mother to him, used, mute, her mind and soul scoured clean.

They escaped the city, then the camps, finally the country.

The horses drift over, ears erect: Is something up?

Do unto me, their eyes say.

"I simply do not understand," Sirut says.

The horses stir, then drift back to their grazing. Long necks arc, the big heads' extravagant lips fuss and ruffle the grass.

"Sirut," she says. "Tell me what was convenient before."

Bliss

All my life, I seem to have been mistaken for someone else. The other day, a woman stopped me in the produce aisle at the market and said, "Michael?" When I pick up heart pills for my dad, the pharmacist always says, "Hi, Tim." When I correct him, he smiles and says, "Good to see you." When I walk down Idle Road from my apartment to my job, or along the highway, people I don't know wave at me from cars. I wave back, it can't hurt. One day a girl leaned out of a car as it shot by and yelled, "I love you, Jamie!" I am introduced to people over and over again. "Have we met?" they say. "It's Walter, or Phil, or Daniel, isn't it?" I have wondered if wearing a name tag would be a bad idea. *Hello, I'm Cleave.* Who could forget such a name? When I look in the mirror I realize that I am, to some extent, a fabrication. The face looks like mine, all right, but also looks, vaguely, like anyone's: a racial cameo of smooth skin, fine hair. Mouth, nose, and eyes all where they should be, but somehow indistinct—the anonymous, undeclared face of a baby. A face you could put a face onto, including your own, or that of someone close to you whom you've not seen in you can't remember how long. *"Michael?"* When the lady in the store said that, I just smiled and shook my head—and she looked confused, hurt, angry. Who had she lost? *Yes,* I wanted to say, but didn't. *Yes, it's me.*

I stepped from the mud and rain of my midday duties into the outer sanctum of the Pritchard Publishing Company. It isn't what people think. No one ever says to me, *Oh*—you work for a *publisher*, because everyone around here knows that there is only one such outfit in this part of the state and that it is owner-operated by the crazy Pritchards, purveyors of four-color brochures to the attractions of the Green Mountains. It's a reprint operation. Mr. Pritchard is our only "author." *Oh*, folks are more likely to say. You work for *them*.

And there is nothing glamorous about what I do: I am the "general help."

When I came in, Mrs. Goodell, our executive secretary, blinked her smartly made-up martyr's eyes at me in a code I could not interpret. She held up her heavily ringed hands; silver bangles rattled into the sleeves of her red blazer. Mr. Pritchard was burning up the telephone in the inner sanctum. "I can't stand this," Mrs. G. said. But I knew that she could. "And Cleave," she added in a register of confidence and woe, "I have to tell you, there are no checks today."

"Excuse me?" I said.

One of my jobs is to take paychecks to Billy and Jill, who make runs to the printer and distribute our materials. They usually hang out at the warehouse on Idle Road, minutes from here but far from here, if you know what I mean. Naturally, it registered that Mrs. G. meant *my* check, too, and I went into meditation mode, or tried to— not easy, what with Jack Pritchard ordering his daughter, LeeAnne, in a voice normally reserved for summoning Satan, to bring him the *receivables*, and she screaming that she could not find them and had he forgotten that receivables were not her *bailiwick*?

Their offices are two doors apart.

Nevertheless, I willed an interior stillness, visualized the cosmos within, and ascended: I looked down on the building, then rose higher, floating over the local greenery, then the county, the state— and on and on in a series of diminishing images until the earth disappeared in the litter of space and I approached the peace and quiet of infinite distance with its cool, clean open-ended light-years.

Someone spoke my name.

I opened my eyes. Mrs. Goodell was looking at me with concern. "Cleave, are you all right?"

"Mrs. G.," I said, "I'm fine. But I do need to be paid."

"You will be paid." Her face darkened with anger. "We will *all* be paid."

I first encountered the Goodells years ago, when I was waiting on tables in a restaurant in the next village. As I made the rounds of my station, I saw that *Mr.* Goodell was in something like a drunken coma. I'd never seen anyone that paralyzed. On a return trip from the kitchen, I glanced at *Mrs.* Goodell, and her face wore the look of concerned and painful anger I was seeing now.

Mr. Pritchard called to me from the inner sanctum. As I entered, he turned his attention from the window and pointed at a package lying on his desk. "Take that to the post office, then go over to the warehouse and tell Billy to close up." The telephone rang, but Mr. Pritchard just ignored it. He ignored me as well: his chair pivoted silently back to the window, to which watery view he appeared to surrender himself. From her office, LeeAnne yelled, "Dad, pick up!" But Mr. Pritchard did not pick up. For a few moments, he and I watched the rain paint the windowpanes.

I made myself ask him about the checks. A glimmering light washed pale shadows down the length of his face. "Cleave," he said, as the phone continued to ring, "please just go."

This is how I met Jill:

Once upon a long time ago, the eighth grade boys and girls were herded indoors for one of their foul-weather-Friday dances. A record player was set up, loafers and sneakers sprinkled onto the hardwood floor, and the musk of dead basketball games warmed and rose. When the needle dropped on the slow and baritonic Righteous Brothers, the boys rushed the girls, who had gathered into ranks of self-defense and availability. I grabbed Jill's hand, led her out among the other dancers, and pressed her to me, and she was not reluctant. I had never held a girl—I had never even held hands with a girl—and here I was all but fused to one. We two-stepped in a small circle without speaking until the Brothers announced one last time that that lovin' feeling was gone. "Thank you, Cleave"—

she breathed these words into my ear. You know how that feels? We peeled apart and cool air rushed between us.

But for some reason, we never clicked, and I didn't do anything to make it happen, and that togetherness—that little knot—untied. There was nothing left on the line but a murmur.

Now, Jill popped out of the warehouse and waved as I drove in, and my heart just laughed like it always does when I see her. "Cleave!" she called. The payday party had begun—she had a bottle of beer in her hand—so I quickly broke the news about the checks. They didn't seem too surprised that we'd been stiffed.

"This bites, man," Billy said. "Cleave: cigarette me." I complied, and he glared at me with rage and affection.

A large, oblong man, top-heavy and uncomfortably hinged, Billy had spent eighteen years in the navy, wandered home to Ohio, where he had a series of adventures involving law enforcement personnel, and now, as manager of the Pritchard Publishing warehouse—a glorified garage—shoved a beer into my hand.

Jill leaned against a stack of shrink-wrapped tourist guides and sipped. Her expression suggested that she was surveying the map of a week without money. In my own mind, phantom digits blinked in and out of existence. Billy wandered in a deliberate slouch, his shoulders braced for battle and for surrender. Then he boiled up, shoving his lizard-skin boot against a stack of pallets, spilling them. "Bastards!" Whipping his empty bottle against the far wall, he reached into the front-loader for a fresh one. Jill scooted past me, grinning madly, hooking my arm into hers, and we escaped.

Now, despite the fact that we'd never gotten to know one another early on, we did get into the habit, years after our school days, of taking walks together. At that time, Jill was seeing someone— in fact, she was informally engaged. But she and Bud (not his real name) were having a serious problem. I got wind of this, and one day I happened to stop in front of her house. She came out—she'd love to take a walk!—and so it became a now-and-again routine: I happened by, and if she happened to be around, we took a walk.

We reviewed the school lives we'd barely shared. She offered me bits and pieces of the Bud problem, and I ate her words like candy. I listened, I nodded gravely, I suggested different routes we could take—riverbank? graveyard? fairgrounds?—and occasionally threw in my two cents' worth. I imagined she might take a different path with Bud, and that my capacity as tour guide might somehow evolve into, simply, guide, and then to something better. But it didn't.

And for a while, all was well. And then it wasn't.

I hung around out front on that fateful December afternoon for what seemed a longer than usual time, and finally she hurried out, head-down, quick in her big boots. I noticed the light jacket and the speculative look she shot my way, and I thought, Well, this is the last time. A guide knows.

"God, it's cold," she informed me. I remarked that it must be polar air riding on the jet stream, and she nodded without looking up and hugged herself more tightly. She said, "Maybe we could just go around the block today."

"Excellent idea," I said. "A walk around the old block."

"Because it's just so *cold* today."

"Do you want to go back? Not that we've gone anywhere."

"What's wrong?"

"How's Bud?" I said.

She stopped right there. "What are you talking about?"

I said, turning to her, "Bud is back in time for the holidays, right? *Bud* has had a change of heart. Right? There will be an announcement on, oh, let me think now, Christmas Eve. Right?" I hated myself for talking this way, and even though it turned out to be true— right down to the impending Christmas Eve joy fest—I felt like a bastard, steamed up and shaking semi-righteously inside my coat. Jill's green eyes glazed. Fingers of wind smoothed strands of hair across her face. Her hair—how can I describe this? There's a ripple effect the wind can't make or unmake. But I went on talking as if I'd spent my whole life making women cry.

"So why are we even—*shit*. What is even the point? You don't have to walk with me, or tell me about *Bud* and Bud's *history* and Bud's *problems*. I don't actually give a good goddamn about Bud, or whatever his name is. I never liked the son of a bitch anyway."

"Well, what *do* you give a damn about? Goddamn it." Her long, fine red nose was pointed right at my chest. And now she was crying openly and swearing, and who, in truth, doesn't love this in a woman? But of course there was only one answer to her question: *You.* But I couldn't say it.

She said, I thought I could talk to you.

She said, I thought you cared.

She said, I thought you were different.

Then she turned and ran back to her house. I did a forced march till my legs started to shake, sucked up a second wind, and continued on out of the village by way of the thruway overpass, where I gripped the empty squares of the anti-suicide chain-link fence and looked down on the cars. Senseless, soulless fools, I thought—the way you do when you're miserable and other people's lives seem abstract, their trajectories pointless. I walked on across the bridge and into a turnout where I found a path that opened on a clearing where the milkweed pods saw a real fool coming and nodded their hairy chins in cold agreement. The moon rose over the mountain and I lay down on the body of the dead earth and watched the rimed and frozen sky turn its back on the day, and my fingers and ears sang and stung with perfect, blissful pain.

What happened was, we didn't exactly make up—how could we make up when we were never together? But I continued to happen to walk by her house, and one day out she came. But I could tell—by the way she eased the door shut, and then by the way my heart turned over once and lay still—that she had *news* for me. She put her arm through mine.

She said that she and Bud were getting married.

She said that things were really fine at last.

She said that she was happy.

It's hard to be angry when someone who will never walk with

you again, or love you in the way you want to be loved, or roll over in the morning and look into your eyes and say, "Why don't you fix me a cup of coffee?" is smiling at you. Isn't that hard? And that was that.

And of course, things were *not* really fine, but that was her business.

But look at us *now*, as they say.

We walked away from the warehouse arm in arm, up Idle Road in the rain, not talking much, and not about money when we did talk. There were other jobs. Her breast caressing my arm had put me into a trance in which I saw the two of us living together in the zero gravity of the space station, sipping iced coffee through straws and enjoying a sunrise every couple of hours, performing important experiments in the common sense of outer space, linking our two souls and bodies and lives. Making up for every day we'd missed down below, where even the air pushes you around.

So we walked along through this scattershot October rain. She told me about a birthday party she'd had for Dylan, her four-year-old—and she asked me what I remembered about being a kid.

"When I was four," I said, "I used to lie in the grass by the side of our house and look up at the sky and feel the sun. Or, other times, it looked like a big messed-up bed with gray sheets—like today. And I could see the drops falling from far up there, and imagined someone wringing out those sheets. God? I don't know. I didn't know where the sky began. I still don't." I spread my arms and put my face into the rain—and the memory of my mother hit me hard. "My mom would run out and scoop me up. I've been happy other times, but I was completely happy then. However—"

I would have liked to bring my hands together, right then, to send a prayer out to my mother's spirit, but they had ideas of their own, and covered my face.

"However," I managed to finish, "I'm completely happy *now*."

I waited through some painful moments, as we set out again, expecting Jill to say something nice and soothing and less than personal that would let me know that I was still the tour guide and should stick to the book. "Well, that's good," is all she said, pulling a little closer to me in a perfect docking maneuver, and I played those three words through every aural filter I had on board. *Bud*—father of little Dylan, but now banished forever from their lives—floated along beside us in spirit, but I just nodded to his troubled, truculent ghost and then ignored it, the way a man does when he knows what matters and what doesn't.

≈

I left the truck with Jill at the warehouse and walked over to West Mountain Road to check on my dad. I went in, calling, then out through the kitchen to the backyard, where he spends time when he's feeling well and the weather's nice. He was there, sitting on the bench between the two maples—"Cleave maples," my mother used to call them, because Dad planted them when I was born.

I'd come along when they had stopped believing any children were going to show up—Dad was past fifty and Mom was forty-three when I was born—and they seemed never to get over the fact that I'd arrived. In family pictures they hold up baby Cleave the way a farmer holds up a monster zucchini. *We didn't really expect this.*

Then Mom got leukemia—like you'd catch a cold or a chill, or fetch a bus up over the curb—and it ran her down, one-two-three. Just about the last time she left the house was for my high school graduation. She then went back into the hospital to see if the doctors could detain the life that was rushing to get out of her as if her body was on fire, and then she came home to die in the house she and Dad had lived in together, and where I've lived, on and off, since appearing on the planet.

As I approached the shaded bench, I saw that Dad's eyes were closed under the brim of the world's dirtiest cap. Asleep or meditating?—I slowed my step. His eyes flicked open to glazed slits, spied me, and instantly closed again, but his face blinked into a smile.

"Come on and sit down, Cleave." Voice as soft as an old shirt.

"How are you, Dad?"

"Oh—the same." He looked at me vaguely, and I knew that he had been asleep. "You're off early?"

"I think I lost my job today. I don't know what's up, but the checks weren't ready. Something's going on."

"Jack Pritchard still running the place?"

"Sure."

He shifted his weight with care. "I'm not surprised," he said. "I knew him when he was a kid."

"You knew everybody when they were a kid."

I followed his gaze up to the house where, in other days, my mother had hummed some bit of a song to distract herself from the kitchen chores she tolerated; and I recalled her whispering in the weeks before she died, "Cleave, I'm just so *tired*," a look of surprise in her face that was mostly bright, panicked eyes by then. She had never seemed tired to me, and now her life was draining from an opened tap into the bottomless bucket of the universe. I recalled how my father read to her as she drifted in and out of sleep, how he'd sometimes crawled into the bed and held her till she woke. I walked long distances in those days, past exhaustion, to where the stars flickered at noon.

When I looked again, his eyes were closed. "Time to go in?"

His smile blinked on. "Plenty of time."

"You're a goddamned old Buddha."

"I'll Buddha you." He opened his eyes. "Who's that girl you've been seeing?"

"What girl? Do you want me to move back in?"

"You think I need a nurse? What's the girl's name?"

"Jill," I said—in an unguided moment.

Dad turned his face back to the house. He removed his cap and pushed crooked fingers through his hair, then screwed the cap back on. He looked unaccountably sad. "Pretty name," he said.

That night I reviewed my day and concluded, in the inflexible diction of darkness, that I had less reason to be hopeful than I'd imagined. Jill's face was there—it held the lambent brightness of a candle's flame—but the image wavered as if a veil of water hung between us. I seemed to be in the street. Then I was standing in front of her house. I walked into the yard, not knowing for sure which window was hers. But I picked one that seemed likely and sat down in the grass beneath it. The night was not cold, so I lay back to smoke and look at the stars. The stars were all smiles. *We got you here*, they seemed to say. *Now what?* Far down the interstate, a big truck plied its gears in a ghostly, diminishing progression of power chords. As I watched the stars, they worked loose and began shooting around the heavens; some streaked down, striking the earth silently, their massive energy flowing into the ground. Jill's face, upside down, looked over the sill at me; her smiling eyes glittered like sickle moons. Drawn to her, I righted myself and put my arms out to her—but she held out a package to me. Two men stood behind her in the darkness of the room. I backed away from my balked desire and the room's threatening shadows, the energy of the subterranean star-flow ran into my feet and coursed through my body, and I rose into the sky.

When I awoke, a voice was speaking my name in the dark. A soft voice, like a woman's, pressing gently but insistently against me. It was so sweet-sounding and so clear that I sat up, startled, and said, "Yes?" But the enticing voice was gone. I got up and made coffee and sat at my little table in the first light, and when I stopped thinking about anything, the presence returned. When I felt it enter the room, I closed my eyes and waited. I raised my hands in supplication.

The presence pressed against me like a wind that doesn't blow.

Then it opened me like an envelope.

When I got to work, there were two shiny state troopers' cars sitting in the lot, one empty, the other discharging a trooper. He met me at the corner of the building.

"Are you Cleave Noone?"

"Yes, sir," I said. "Please don't shoot."

"That's not funny, Mr. Noone."

"No, sir, I'm sorry. Long night."

Several people were paying attention from a little distance. A woman wearing wraparound sunglasses loitered intensely with coffee and a cigarette. "They'd like to talk to you inside," the trooper said.

A couple of the spectators slipped their orbits and wobbled toward us. The coffee-and-cigarette lady, feeling the love, took a step into the street. This seemed not unsafe, but distances, in space, are deceiving. And I felt an odd compression—a condensation of cold words—filling my ears.

"If you would just step inside," the trooper said.

As I approached the outer sanctum, I beheld a tableau: Mrs. Goodell huddled in her honest cloth coat; LeeAnne Pritchard, in a blue jogging suit, crouched beside her, speaking low; and at the edge of the frame a heavy man wearing a nouveau-sharkskin suit. I came closer and both women looked up into my headlights, so to speak.

"What's going on?" I said.

"Who is this?" the shark hissed.

Pale LeeAnne inch-wormed upright, ignoring him. "Well, well," she said. "You're a little late today, Cleave."

"You didn't have to call the police," I said.

"LeeAnne," said the man, "I'm asking you not to talk to anyone right now."

"He's just the janitor," she said. "Well, how about it, Cleave? Did you make out last night?"

Mrs. Goodell stood up so quickly that her chair threw itself into a filing cabinet. "This young man is Cleave Noone," she said in a voice that suggested I was about to be knighted, or sent to prison. She turned a look of concerned and painful anger on LeeAnne. "And I am going home now."

"Oh—great," LeeAnne said as Mrs. Goodell swept through the door. "That's just *great*. Why don't we all just *go home*."

"It's what I would do," I said, "only I've just come from there."
The hard stuff in my ears had begun to crumble, and sounds were
sprinkling onto the floor of my mind, where Jill swept them into a
pile. "What's going on?"

At that moment, the door to the inner sanctum opened and Jack
Pritchard emerged. He marched straight past me and entered into
communion with LeeAnne and the shark. A trooper and another
man came to the door of the office, and I was beckoned inside.

The other man—a detective—wanted to know all about my job.
This took about three minutes. He then nodded to the trooper.
Through a miracle of modern communication, this trooper had
learned from his partner that I'd said I'd had a late night. The detective turned to me.

How late, Cleave? *Very.* How come? *I lost track of the time.* What
does that mean? *You tell me.* Couldn't you sleep? *Nope.* Did you go
out? *I—No.* Did you see anyone? *I was completely alone.* Are you sure
you didn't go out? *What is this?* What is what? *This.* Was—he looked
down at his notebook—Billy with you at any time yesterday? *I saw
him at the warehouse.* Were you drinking? *I had a beer.* Do you often
drink on the job? *Only on paydays, which yesterday wasn't.*

"Why was that, Cleave?"

"You tell me."

The lines on the detective's face had been bent into sadness by
the gravity of too many lies. "Okay, Cleave, I will. We believe that
someone broke into this office some time last night or early this
morning. Do you know anything about that?"

"I don't."

"Okay. Do you know where we might find Billy?"

"The last I saw Billy, he was at the warehouse. Okay? I went for
a walk with Jill—is this what you wanted to know?"

"Sure."

"When we got back, I left the truck—"

At this point, I remembered the package Mr. Pritchard had asked
me to mail—and I remembered last night: surely these were the
men standing in Jill's room in my dream? *You left this in the truck,*

she had said then. In my mind, now, she swept the debris of words into a small box.

"I don't know what's in the package—the box—I don't know anything." And I got up to leave.

The trooper was in front of me instantly. "Whoa, whoa, whoa. Take a seat, Mr. Noone."

"What package, Cleave?" the detective said.

My legs gave way, and I sat down hard. "I didn't ask to fucking come here," I said.

"Okay," the detective said. "What package, Cleave?"

"And I didn't see that crazy son of a bitch after that, either."

"Who's that, Cleave?"

"BILLY." I was out of time. "I did not ask to come here."

"Okay, Cleave. Cleave?"

I had to laugh then, because suddenly I was standing by the window—a space walk. And I missed it! The detective was looking distinctly nervous and I wanted to reassure him, but what came out of my mouth was an alien language of groans and slurs and shushes. Words that weren't words fumbled from my lips and fell to the floor like stricken bees. Something inside me was bent; something that was kinked needed to be straightened out, but stretching my arms out the window until my fingers touched the stars didn't help. The stars had worked loose again and spilled like sparks over a sky that held the hard, flaring blue of sheet metal pressed against the sun. The men were pulling me back into the room. Then, looking up, I saw a watermark crusted high up on the walls, just beneath the ceiling. "This is a room that has flooded before," I said, but did they hear me? Did they understand that all that is integrated will be dissolved? I let them do what they would. I hadn't asked to come here. And as the level of the water rose, I took back everything I had ever said or done or been, and the rest abandoned ship. Even the presence, occupying my last hiding place—the whole of me, just under the skin—left me. The universe darkened down to an infinitely small box Jill held out, whose angles enfolded, comforted, and silenced me, and held me fast.

≈

The rule about the locked ward seemed to be that you could talk or you could listen, but if you did neither, they kept you there until you did *something*. They needed clues, too.

Brought before a panel of whitecoats, I was awarded a medal for psychotic tendencies under dissociative conditions and moved to a ward where I was blended with the run-of-the-mill sick. I rose like thick, quiet cream, was scooped into a bed discreetly equipped with the hardware of restraint—fortunately not needed—and in my idleness got to know the nursing staff, rattling off *LindaCecilia MaryanneSally* inside the empty barrel of my head. This between naps brought on by doses of some very nice stuff that came through a needle and turned out my lights.

Mostly, I lay back and looked through a glassy rectangle at late, cold October, and drifted.

My very own psychiatrist came by once a day, or I shuffled through the traffic to his office. "So, what happened?" he asked me right off—eager beaver. "Any place is the right place," he added, meaning I should spill it. A box of Kleenex hunkered between us. *Weep, damn you!* I appreciated his patter and the fact that, like me, he seemed to know a lot more than he was telling. We got along. I'd fall into the water and he'd fish me out, and then we'd talk about what being wet was like. After a week of this, he said, "Don't you think it's time to go home?" "Fuck you," I replied, even though I was not particularly angry. "And the horse you rode in on." "What's that about, Cleave?" he asked.

It was about him being my age, and not crazy.

Dad came and went. They'd brought in a decent chair so he could be comfortable. I turned my head and there he was. *Blink.* "Hey," I said.

"Hey, yourself. How are you?"

I fumbled my way through dozy synapses, but couldn't discover what was wanted, so I just returned the question.

"Well, Cleave," he said, "not so good. Everything takes so long. I have breakfast, then I lie down for a little. What's the point of that?" He reached to turn on the lamp. "The doctor says you took a little break from reality—more than a little. This room is all right, is it?"

"I'm ready to say good-bye to it. I feel older than you. Stop fussing." He was picking at the tower of flowers Mrs. G. had had delivered. I continued, ungratefully, "I want to go home."

"Well, you can't go home today. Which reminds me, that girl came by and I gave her the key to your place." He closed his eyes. "Nice girl."

"What *girl*? Jill?"

"Mmm. We had a nice talk."

"So—what are you telling me? You were hitting on Jill? That's unseemly."

"I'll unseemly you."

Nurse-errant Sally came in, bearing her wonderful little needle. "Time to rest," she said. "You can stay if you like, Mr. Noone. He'll be out, though."

"Just pretend like I'm not here," I said. "It's what *I* do."

"All right, now, hon, roll onto your side for me."

Dad rose and pulled on his coat. "I'll be going. Be good, and do what they tell you. As if you wouldn't. I'll see you tomorrow." He dithered at the foot of the bed. When Sally gave me the needle he turned away, cranking his cap on.

"So when is she coming to see me?"

"Hell should I know?" he muttered.

"What's your problem, old-timer?"

"Don't have one. Maybe if you were a little less . . . seemly, you wouldn't have to ask me what you should already know."

"Is that right?"

"Damn right it's right." He dithered some more, but with less attitude, then moved back to the side of the bed. The nurse marked my chart and left, and Dad sank into his chair again. I didn't know what to make of his mood, and I struggled against the drug that was pulling at my sleeve—*right this way, sir*—as the last leaves of light fluttered over his shoulders.

"Dad?"

"Hmm?"

"Stay a while, would you?"

≈

Dad's restless in the middle of the night. He calls out at two in the morning, a cry with words wrapped in it. By the time I make it in there from where I've nodded off on the couch and switch on the bedside light, he's sitting up, staring with wild eyes. I smooth down his covers and ease him back onto the pillow. "I think I'll stay over tonight and babysit," I say, hoping to get a smile, but he just closes his eyes obediently, and I feel rebuked. But I stay fewer and fewer nights at my place.

On my first day home, I'd discovered that *Star Trek* is on every night of the week. But the closing theme gusting up behind a close-up of the bemused Captain Kirk just kicked my ass. I slept, when I could. I stood at the west-facing window in the afternoons and watched the stars glimmer on.

The note Jill left me on the night table lay curled like a little paper hand on the palm of which were the words *Call me.*

Finally, I give up the apartment. Without a job, I can't afford to keep the place, anyway. I move in with Dad and begin looking for work, making my way down through the layers of labor until I hit bottom at the HangUps coat hanger plant on Connector Street. But they're down to seventeen employees, from forty-three, and half the workers have carpal tunnel. It's a sad place. The foreman hands me an application form and asks, a little too loudly, if I didn't used to work at Pritchard's. I give him the short version of what Mrs. Goodell told me when, still simmering, she came to see me in the hospital.

"Jack was in terrible trouble—the business was failing. *I* didn't know a *thing*," she said. "He jerry-rigged the books and took out a loan. Then he cashed in whatever he could and made it look like the office had been burglarized."

"You don't say."

"Yes! The package poor Billy stole was full of cash."

"Who sends cash through the *mail*?" I felt a loony laugh coming up fast. I had already read about Billy being picked up. It seems he'd been heading due south but got sidetracked. In his haste to reach an ocean, he rear-ended a police car in downtown Providence, and when the officers got out, he did too, and ran, briefly, away. "Was LeeAnne involved?"

"That little bitch." Mrs. G. shook her bangles with a shaman's briskness. "Don't laugh, Cleave. Like father, like daughter. Now, settle down. They tell me you're going home today. What will you do?"

Through my tears, I said, "I thought I'd retire."

But the HangUps man just shrugs and shows me the door. I try to walk through it as little like a mental patient as possible.

~

Deciding to loosen up, I throw away my Paxil and feel better (I think) immediately. January thaw helps—who minds being made a fool of at midwinter?—and so does walking. The schedule of classes taped to the door of the Eight Smiles High yoga studio tells me to bring myself and ten dollars on Monday afternoon, and on the day, I roll out my mat and await instructions. The studio's in a corner of an old factory, and stern light sits up straight in the tall windows. Cathy, the teacher, modulates the stereo's wood-flute-and-whale song and I attempt to do as she asks, bending and unbending myself discreetly. "Form an intention for your practice today," she tells us. "Breathe." More specific, but puzzling, instructions follow. "Locate your abdominal muscles. Find your shoulder blades." By the end of the hour, I'm tired and cranky. I throw my mat into the basket and go home.

The next sessions are better. I can't stretch, breathe, or bend with anything like intention, but I fake it until something like intention happens. I attempt a simple mountain pose—arms up, hipbones floating over the feet, spine stretching—and wonder if my neck is supposed to hurt this much. Cathy circulates in my direction, then steps up to my mat and touches the small of my back. "Drop your butt," she says softly. "Let your shoulders go. Feel your feet. Press those index fingers through the ceiling." She observes my effort. "And *breathe*, Cleave."

We end the hours lying on our backs in corpse pose. "Practice," Cathy smiles, "for the day when we'll stop breathing." I want to hear this? An Eastern bell's note goes on and on. Cathy drifts above us, turning off the lights until only one lamp is left burning. Layers of denser shadow wash over my eyelids; my backbone comes close to being one with the mat. When the session ends, I sit up slowly, reluctantly, and breathe deeply. *Bonnnnng, (bo(bong)nnngg)* goes the bell. Nothing hurts. I breathe again, pull on my socks and hold on to my feet. Again, tears. And a snake of joy hustles through me at a crazy angle.

The following week, I bring Dad. He's a big hit. He finds his shoulder blades right away. He immediately has three or four girl-friends, middle-aged women who can't pay enough attention to him. He buys a CD from Cathy. That night, whales sing while we have dinner, and we grin at one another across the table. We both start sleeping better.

Then one night I awaken to the sound of a voice, soft as a woman's, speaking my name. It comes again and I follow the sound to his bedroom. "Did you call me?"

"No," he says, bewildered. His eyes glisten in the fall of light from the hallway. Then: "Yes. Yes, I heard it, too, Cleave."

~

The sky is hard and bright after a brief, early shower of snow. By the time I leave the house, the storm clouds have moved into the east, and I follow these ghosts as far as Jill's house, where I pause to knock on the door. I hold my breath—then I breathe. The door opens.

She says she is glad to see me.

She says she'd love to go for a walk.

She tells me she's been wondering about me.

We walk through the village and then out of it, passing the hang-er plant, where the workers having a smoke on the loading dock raise their braced and bandaged forearms to return our greeting.

The wind bears down, blowing our breath back down the hill as we cut across Idle Road and walk up through a development of newer houses. To the top, where the street ends in a cul-de-sac and barren plots slotted with driveways await the promised homes. Turning, we look down on the way we've come. The broad roofs of the split-levels and capes and ranches glimmer like the blades of a magnificent mobile, but all that moves is the wind.

Vanishing World

I work small, with brush and paint, knives and files, a scalpel, wire and solder, a magnifying glass, sandpaper, every kind of cloth, string and fabric, and the sound, somewhere back in the distance of my mind and memory, of a train whistle.

We were barely two generations of miniaturists; after me, there's no one. And we were a big family, at least by the non-Catholic west Connecticut standards of the day, Catholic meaning six to eight kids in worn-out sweaters and the day being that season between the whitewashed housing project of the early fifties and the happy slum of 1969.

Four kids: Michele, me, and the twins, Eve and Peggy, who became the business's expert tree painters—what Dad called mock-flockers. Of all our tedious jobs, the one that accounted for a third of our man-, woman-, and child-hours. Sitting and chatting together, breathless, pauseless, the twins could settle a Christmasy snow on the branches of a miniature spruce forest in about the time it takes nature to do the same in the larger sphere. In our basement shop, boxes and rows and groves and shelves-full and forests of mock-flocked trees glimmered in the moon's-glow of a night light all spring and summer, waiting on the orders of October.

≈

Eve and Peggy: Mom's little mid-thirties surprise party. They didn't add to the family, they redefined it, the way a hailstorm reckons with a car. Dad handed out orders to Michele and me while in the

upper reaches of the house the storm raged. The girls began talking (to each other) at the breast, one offering loud encouragement
while the other suckled. They did their best to defy Mother's gravity, but her pepper-and-cream Irish prevailed—just. She pulled them
down to earth, got them on their feet, ran them to ground. Their
lights went out nightly at eight; they fell as if stricken and slept as
if comatose. We approached their crib with the loony reverence of
UFO watchers: *Could they be real? What did they want?* "They need
to grow up," Dad growled. "We're getting behind."

We called him the Chief.

The Chief announced at the dinner table that he'd decided to mod-
ernize the shop. He dished scalloped potatoes onto Peggy's plate.
"Don't everyone talk at once," he said. Mom diddled her fork in a
puddle of sauce, the smile she usually ran up at such announcements caught at half-mast. Michele and I exchanged looks. I figured
life was hard enough without overtime, and even though Dad paid
us, fumbling fives and tens from his pockets as he calculated aloud
our weekend and after-school hours, I saw small towns in my sleep.
Sometimes, in my dreams, canal-side villages burned to the water-
line. Other times I walked weightless as lint and voiceless as a fly
through the rooms of tiny, empty, silent stations.

The Chief and I studded the basement, walled off the furnace and
carpeted an area beneath the stairs he'd designated Staff Lounge. We
hung a false ceiling, installed a table saw he'd rebuilt, and set new,
larger fluorescent trays over the work tables—and then he said he
wanted to add a bar. Michele popped her eyes and twirled a crazy-
circle finger at her temple, and the twins did whatever Michele did,
so there seemed to be a consensus. I looked him in the eye and delivered the most devastating line I knew: "You're kidding, right?"
Mother—whose architectural ambitions had been siphoned into
the family business before you could say, *I spent four years in college
for this?*—hit the stairs. "I'd never kid a kidder, my boy," the Chief
said, with his eye on Mom's exit.

We went at it for three days. With a lackey's compliance, I endured his pictographic and inspired instructions—there were no plans—shaped and fitted Formica, cut and re-cut and measured mahogany and pine and held tools while he fussed the plumbing into a miracle of cooperation. On break in the Lounge, I chewed to death the sandwiches Michele brought down. I was fifteen, and my soul ached. The twins shouted like gulls through the gate at the top of the stairs. Mother sang something French in the kitchen. A false ceiling, I fumed. *False!* And now this!

When we were finished, it looked like a really nice bar into which someone had brought work tables and benches. Our shop space had actually been reduced. Mom chattered that it looked *fine*. Michele laughed. The twins laughed.

⁓

At the end of the day, Dad would announce he was knocking off, then he'd stroll across the room to the bar, build a drink, and climb onto a barstool. But the little world impinged on this new space just as it had long since crept into the upstairs rooms. The back bar was lined with houses, sheds and poles, radio towers, groves of the aforementioned spruce forest, and odd bits of paraphernalia, the stuff you couldn't buy out of a catalog and for which we were known: a bucket so small its contents wouldn't fill a thimble, tin-shiny, with a printed paper label and an eyelash-fine brush frozen in its drop of red enamel; a half-rusted tricycle with wedding ring–sized whitewall tires; Michele's silkscreened or painted signs and banners and billboards, their perfection skillfully marred with tea, plaster dust, and spit; the Chief's houses, so perfect—so much better, apparently, than the real thing—that they brought tears to clients' eyes; Mother's hand and eye over and under all, shaping, defining, foundational; my wiring, lighting, plumbing—my doing whatever needed doing—and the girls' trees, shrubs, grasses, gardens. Tumbleweeds. Dead limbs, rusty confetti-piles of oak leaves. Cemetery bouquets colorless, stiff, and dry.

⁓

Michele's bedroom was hipness itself. Eve and Peggy (as they got older), Mrs. Claus the cat, and the occasional slumming parent—less often Dad, who seldom left the shop—all wound up there from time to time. Lying on Michele's bed, the twins sipped coffee from demitasse—just the thing for their unevolved but tap-dancing nervous systems—and sang along with Michele's Dylan records. Michele brooded over them in a swishy kimono, and in turn they wrapped themselves in towels and fashioned their hair into slithery bumps into which they stuck pencils. When the parents finally banned coffee absolutely and attempted to snuff out the early, querulous Dylan, Michele substituted mint tea and played Dad's Nat Cole: anything to please. The somewhat quieted twins slipped around the house in their off-hours in velvet-topped flip-flops, chanting together in a low, faux-Oriental lingo. They wouldn't use forks and couldn't use chopsticks. Drove Mother crazy.

We didn't give them nostalgia. "They want the good old days, they can read a book," Dad said of the clients. He didn't read much himself except mechanical trades magazines and *Popular Mechanics*; didn't take time off, didn't believe in leisure, idleness, or speculation. He would, from time to time, take one of his pipes out of the drawer, fire it up, and walk around the house trailing an acrid cloud of English blend. Like ducklings, the twins followed, quacking. Mother coughed and opened windows. Michele liked the aroma, she said: it was "manly." The Chief puffed up and down the stairs with his pipe in his teeth, his normal pace halved. "Dad, what are you thinking about?" I asked him once—an impulsive question that left us both aghast. He looked at me with wide, bland eyes. "Nothing."

Life was not so strange. The twins had their friends over. In tenth grade, Michele had a boyfriend, Willie, who came in after school and sat on the sofa like a stone. You wanted to hold a mirror to his nostrils. I had friends, too, all of them curious: What went on at our house? I took them down for the tour. Dad looked up, scowled. He put them to work—anything simple—Mother fed them, and they went away. But clients never came to the house. Dad worked the phone and wrote letters, his Remington solid as a cinderblock on the bar, his drink jumping with the pounding of the keys. Strangely enough, the orders—and the money—came in.

But all was not well.

≈

Mother, who had been flickering on and off our radar screen for a couple of weeks, came in one afternoon and began banging around the kitchen. I wandered in there to observe this shift in her style. Michele entered stage left. The twins were partying in the living room. The Chief was out.

Mom took a bottle of white wine from the fridge, dropped ice cubes into a wineglass, sloshed in the wine and took a drink. She took out a knife, a package of cut-up chicken, a bag of celery. "You two," she said over her shoulder, "help me get this dinner ready." But before we could leap into action, she turned to face us and her eyes flicked around the room as if she were appraising its value. The look she settled on me suggested she was wondering what I was worth, too. "Johnny. Tell your father we'll eat in less than an hour."

"Bold Eagle meet with client, Mom."

"Oh." She took another slug. "Michele, see if you can do something with those girls."

"Let's have *them* for dinner," I suggested.

"They're fine, Mom." Michele slipped her arm around Mother's shoulders. "Mom, are you all right? You're acting a little weird."

Mother closed her eyes. "I'm all right. I just need—" She opened her eyes. "You two," she said. "What do you know? Nothing. You want to know something? I never thought this would happen. I had some idea, but it wasn't"—she raised her glass as if she were about to propose a toast—"it wasn't this."

The twins screamed and thundered toward the sound of the front door creaking open: The Chief was home.

Michele spoke low. "What is it, Mom?"

But Mother just shook her head vaguely, turned, leaned over, and threw up into the sink.

She's pregnant, I thought. *Again!*

≈

Mother was not pregnant. She was having an affair. With the son of a client.

Mom was a landscape designer, at first in the real world, briefly, where she was one of about fifty of the female variety, and then here at home, in the basement. If you wanted something done small, and you wanted a substantial landscape—hills and water to go with your small-town-whistle-stop—she was the one to make your tiny dream come true. Or the backdrop for your Venusian heliport, or your own Mount Rushmore fashioned into an island whose waters teemed with nineteenth-century Taiwanese fishing vessels. Or whatever. Dad brought in the job, and they discussed it over dinner. He opened and closed the deal, but in between, there was Mother.

Dad: "I got a call from Ed Wexler today."

Mother: "What does *he* want?"

"Well, you know that room they have? Off the living room? With all the windows?"

"A sunroom?" Mom's voice rose to meet the word "sun." She shaded her eyes as if to ward it off.

"That's right, doll, the sunroom."

"Oh, God."

"Okay, now, hon, look: They now have grandchildren. They want it done right."

"River?"

Dad grinned, breaking bread and feeding it by hand to the twins, who were perched on their chairs, pretending to be border collies. "Two," he said. "Two rivers. Or a river and a stream."

"I can't believe I'm even—will you girls stop!" The twins were barking at Mrs. Claus, who was slinking along the wall. "They're going to have to do something about those windows." Mom hated doing water, and she hated natural light. She wanted to be the one to provide the sun and decide if water would flow.

Dad's smile grew to idiot proportions. "I know," he said. "But they won't. They love sunlight. Ed says—"

"Don't tell me: Ed says the setting sun will only add to the charm of the etcetera."

"Yes," Dad said. "Isn't it wonderful? They want us to do it. They want it by Christmas."

During the war, Dad had designed and built models for tanks and airplanes and weapons systems. After the war, he worked for a while for General Motors. But the Chief needed room: One day he walked away from GM, and the next morning he was in the basement, building tables and giving orders to his team.

"Oh, my goodness, they'll have it by *Christmas*," Mother said. "I don't need to actually *have* a life. The children and I will just put our beds downstairs and devote the rest of our days to Ed Wexler and his *sun*room, won't we, children?"

The twins began to bay.

"Could anyone just pass me, like, *anything* to eat?" Michele said.

When Mom went the next day to the Wexlers' to size up the room, she met their son Jeffrey, who, it turned out, was a town planner. It was his kids the grandparents were about to drop eight grand to please. He and Mother talked about the job, the elder Wexlers canoed quietly in and out, wine was poured and Mother, Michele told me later, fell in love while listening to Jeffrey Wexler describe a housing scheme he'd developed for the municipality of Ensenada, Mexico.

The shit hit the fan about six weeks later. Michele and I were relaxing in the Lounge when it happened.

Mother and I had built the Wexlers' lagoon—they wanted more and more water, so we just went all the way—and she'd roughed out, sculpted, and plastered a landscape that approximated the bone structure of a Baja fishing hamlet, the south-of-the-border theme having sort of developed as we worked. In a six-hour sprint, we chopped the waterways, braced and roughly plumbed the works (all in pieces, for transport), and wired it, and then Mother stepped back, stared for a long sixty seconds, and said, "I don't like it."

The Chief was at that moment coming down the stairs. "Don't be silly," he said. The twins clunked down behind him.

"Thank you, I'm not being *silly*." Mother turned from the piece and slung her gloves onto the floor as if ridding herself of stupid hands.

"Some of your best work," Dad said, busy behind the bar. He looked up. "What?"

Michele: "No one said anything, Dad."

"*Oh*. So when I said it was some of your mother's best work, I guess I said it just to hear myself say it."

"Please, Ray."

"No, I mean it." Dad crossed to the shop with his drink. "Very good. I'll put it this way: One would think almost that you'd been there. Very authentic. I'm sure the Wexlers will be pleased."

Mother stood there with her arms crossed, her Irish way down, frowning into his face. I suddenly wanted to be somewhere else. Michele made a sound and I looked and saw her tears.

"Right here," Dad said, pointing. "Where you have this ridge coming into this greater mass, it's too big. All this is too big. But then you balance it with this hilly thing and a road coming around over here. Nice."

"It's not too big."

"*Bulky* is what I meant, Helen." He spoke harshly. "The proportions. But you've solved it beautifully." The ice tinkled in his glass in the silence. "Wouldn't you say, Johnny? And Michele, if you need a tissue, doll, there are some behind the bar."

"Stop it," Mother said. The twins had placed themselves uncertainly between the parents and turned distressed faces from one to the other.

"Stop what? It's good work. Jeff Wexler will love it. Has he seen it?"

"Please."

"*No?* No private viewing? Not even a sketch? In how many of your long, everlasting fucking afternoon meetings, or should I say, afternoon fuckings? Jesus, Helen, you're slipping! I'd have thought—"

Dad was no good at this. He was shaking so hard, he shimmied.

He walked back over to the bar and set his glass down and put his face in his hands and wept. Michele became a fountain of tears. The twins clung to Mother's legs and howled. Mother sobbed.

"How could you?" Dad cried out. "How?"

"You make me what I am," Mother replied. But she went to him, and they went upstairs together.

A couple of weeks later, Mom and Dad took a little vacation, leaving the twins in Michele's care—not that they needed that much looking after anymore. But we all felt scrambled, breathless. The girls swung with Michele for a week, and her capacity to radiate sunshine was put to the test.

I expected any number of thunderclaps upon their return, but re-entry was uneventful: Dad was smoothly, loudly affectionate, shouting back at the twins, laughing, sticking out a hey-buddy hand for me to shake—which I took, with real happiness. Mom followed, but not right away. Michele dashed outside to meet her, and they came in together a few minutes later, their arms around one another.

Everyone took a big breath. Everyone relaxed. Except the twins.

PART 2

The business has changed. What used to scrape up ten grand in a year now brings ten grand a pop: a split-level Dad raised from eleven ounces of soft- and hardwood sticks, cellophane, plaster, and paint in a week's time is a hot item, and the rich collector is always collecting. My own work, while in demand, naturally brings less. But now and again I act as consultant with the big makers. In the age of virtual wonders, the old stuff is creaky, quaint, and costly—collectible to some, art to others—and I am a minor celebrity, salesman, and spokesman for the good old days.

Which ended when the clients quit coming.

"Where the hell did everybody go?" Dad asked too often, then not often enough, then not at all. He lived on the phone, shout-ing enthusiasm down the wire, pressing old clients for the names of their friends.

The twins slipped out of the workshop, where the thinning for-ests were beginning to collect dust, and into life. But Dad wouldn't allow anything to be covered. ("Get those goddamned sheets off of that work.") We finished 1968 eating out of cans. Mom had tak-en a job landscaping for a local builder and lived in rubber boots, rubbed lotion onto the backs of her roughening hands, smiled. Dad stuck it out downstairs until it was over. We squeaked through Christmas.

On New Year's Day, grim-faced, Dad brought up box after box from the cellar, and he and I loaded a few small towns into the back of the station wagon. Two hours later, he announced he was going into business with a man he knew from the trade—a Mr. Golden, who had a hobby shop in town. He'd bought in with miniature real estate.

The Chief had become a partner.

He and Mom talked about putting the house up for sale.

Michele went to college.

But before all that happened—that and more, to our great sor-row—I went into the navy, where I found lots of trouble waiting for me.

≈

I met Darwin Tolstoy in boot camp. He had not, it turned out, been named after the famous Darwin, but after his grandmother Dar-winia, who had been named after the famous Darwin. A large, shy Minnesota boy, he struggled to keep a low profile, but his name and size were against it. Crouching, he became more, not less, visible, his sleek head and large ears cutting through the lower altitudes, bright eyes shining like anxious headlights. Our company commander, a bitter, middle-aged drunk who hated boots, and especially boots who stood out in any way, called him "Tool Boy," "Toadstool," "Toy-town," and "Toasty."

"Toasty" stuck with the men, in part because it sounded friendly and also because no one knew what to make of Darwin. Was he man or mouse? Brain or retard?

Certainly not the latter: When tapped as company historian, Darwin wrote up two dozen thin, just-add-water personal histories, embellishing and improving the life stories of boys who had had too little life, thus far, to contain much history. He took down the facts on me during one of the company's twice-daily fifteen-minute smoke-and-Cokes.

The air in the smoke-and-Coke room was pure sepia poison. Boots chain-smoked, guzzled Cokes, and shouted. Toasty leaned in to ask a question and after I answered, I asked if I could be his assistant. He replied that he didn't really need one. I said I'd help, anyway. Looking away, he nodded.

Nights after dinner, we sat in a corner of the barracks and worked on the histories, ignoring the general roar. We worked and talked and wrote our letters until lights out and then we went to our bunks. Days, we double-timed the boot-camp routine: rifle range, naval history, fire control. Things slowed down in the mess hall, where the air was dark with the aroma of burned coffee. Darwin and I sat together—sometimes. A caution I'd never known opened its eyes, found mine, and whispered into my ear.

On Christmas Eve, Darwin and me and about ten others from adjacent barracks were volunteered to set up chairs for the following day's ecumenical service in the drill hall, a building so huge it encompassed distinct atmospheres. Carols tinkled down from speakers hidden in literally unseen heights, echo upon breathy echo shivering the air with slivers of thinnest glass. Three thousand folding chairs lay in vast windrows, gleaming in the dim light, along the blocks-long walls. We set about it, resigned to working all night. Darwin and I worked together, gradually moving away from the others, until fields of space lay between us and them. At midnight we drank coffee, discussed the histories, shared an unregulated cigarette, smiled. Looked at one another, smiled, embraced, kissed, and made love, our maneuvers clumsy, urgent, and quick—a liquid, earth-shaking full-body handshake, ears pricking for the sound of voices, my hand over my own mouth to stifle the cry at the moment of climax.

"Tolstoy," I said, holding his big head and looking into his sleepy, brilliant eyes. "Tolstoy, I love you. What should I call you?" We were reclining lumpily on pea coats in a shadowed alcove between two banks of chairs. From a quarter mile away, men's voices mingled icily with the notes of "Silent Night."

Darwin smiled and looked away. "Leo," he said.

~

Because he was too tall to negotiate safely a ship's passageways and hatches, Leo was assigned shore duty at the Naval Air Station on Coronado Island, just over the bridge from where fifty thousand other sailors and myself were kept fresh in the tin cans of San Diego's Pacific Fleet. Overjoyed at our luck in being stationed so close together, we got an apartment in Old Town, ransacked the Goodwill for kitchen stuff and a bed, and spent our weekends on the beach. On weekday mornings I took the bus to the base and at the end of the day, caught a bus home—lots of sailors did. Leo rode a Honda over the Bay Bridge twice a day; on laundry day, toll change rained from all his pockets. When one of us had duty, the other bach'ed it. California was hot, cool, foggy, sunny, cheap, glorious. We lay in the dunes piled at the back of Coronado beach with paperbacks and drank Oly and gazed at the far-off loaf of Point Loma baking in the sun.

One morning on the way to the base, a sailor from my ship—a gunner's mate with whom I had a nodding acquaintance—pushed his way to where I was standing in the aisle.

"Hey, lady," he said.

"Beg pardon?"

He grinned—Swenson was the name—and looked around. "He begs my fucking pardon." He turned back to me. The smile had become a sneer. "I said, 'Hey, lady.'"

"I don't get you." But I did.

Two other men from our ship were sitting nearby. They watched with interest.

"I said, 'Hey, *faggot*.'"

More men became interested. Message delivered, Swenson breathed his dismal breath in my direction and turned away. The bus droned into the base lot, cornering like an old man negotiating ice.

At noon chow I got looks on the mess deck. There was some high school–type snickering. A boatswain's mate name of Henderson followed me into the head after lunch and demanded I go down on him and, when I tried to push past him, knocked me to the deck. Mildly concussed, I made my way to the electronics supply room, let myself in, and sat shaking for ten minutes.

That evening, I told Leo what had happened. "Please, don't," I said, but he was up and out of the apartment. I went after him. We walked twelve blocks and ended up at a Denny's. Leo and I sat opposite each other and I looked at him looking at our coffees. "It'll be okay," I said. "It's nothing. It'll pass." His face was white, he was that scared.

There was no laughter the following day. I saw some stone faces, I saw others that were too happy to see me and too busy to pause. I cruised through my duties in Radar and, spinning out the time, continued through chow—skipped the meal, cursing myself—and finally exited Radar at the end of the day and stood at the railing. A pelican sailed with amazing slowness down, down, and *plooshed!* into the bay.

Leo had duty that night. I ate, watched television, and picked up a magazine. At eleven I called him and was put through. *What?* he said, as if we had a bad connection. *What is it?* "I wanted to make sure you were all right," I said—and felt foolish. *All right? Okay.* I was baffled by the distant tone, the bland wall of words. "Can you talk now?" A pause, then: *All right, then.* And he hung up.

He came in the next morning in a rage. "You can't call me there. Don't *ever* call me there! Are you crazy? I don't answer the phone there, the duty officer answers the phone!"

"So? I'm glad he's doing his duty." I moved in, trying to make light, but he pushed my arms aside.

"These people know—are you crazy? We can't let these people know what we're doing."

"What are we doing?"

"We are *breaking the law.*" He stood with fists clenched, reddening, his Midwestern shabby gentility in tatters.

"I love you." I was spiraling down, every word—even the right ones—wrong.

"You're late," he said. "Go."

After morning muster, I set about replacing a series of relays in a Radar unit. When I returned to the electronics shop, the ship's doctor, a lieutenant commander, was in occupation. He held his hat in his hand as if he'd come to ask a favor—which, in a sense, he had.

In his stateroom, he pushed a paper across the desk. Would I swear to a preliminary finding, pending an investigation, that I was not a homosexual presently cohabiting with another homosexual named Darwin Tolstoy? "We know all about it." He looked sad.

I said I wouldn't sign.

"I wish it were otherwise," he said. "We will have to let you go, John. There are . . . better and worse ways to go about this."

I left the ship and walked down the pier, so dizzy with confusion I lurched. At the apartment, I opened a beer and sat at the kitchen window and looked out into the light of the flawless, changeless California day. When the telephone rang, I seized it.

It was Mother, sobbing. "Johnny, you have to come home. You have to come home now, right away, right now."

~

Late in the afternoon of the October day that Mother, the Chief, and Michele celebrated the twins' sixteenth year, the girls went off to spend the night with one of their friends. We found out later that they didn't stay with the girl, who was a party to the deception, but instead walked over to Route 63 to hitchhike to New Haven to meet up with a boy Eve had met at the beach the previous summer. They planned to return to the friend's house the following day, and then return home—with no one the wiser.

A battered Lincoln pulled up. The driver said he was a musician heading to New York to play a gig. He had some beer in the car and Eve and Peggy shared one—their first. *I've got something better than beer,* he said. *Would you girls like to get high? I always get high before a gig.* Eve said they were all laughing, and then he asked if they'd like to hear a really different kind of song—one of his own—and that she and Peggy said okay. But he didn't sing anything, Eve said. The girls talked to each other for a few minutes, but the silences grew longer, and the car flew along. Then he said, as if talking to himself, *We'll have to be careful.* He pulled the big car off of 63 and on to the road to Peat Swamp Reservoir and then into a dirt pulloff that dissolved into grassy scrub. He shut off the car's engine.

The girls hadn't had much to drink, Eve said, just the one beer between them, and in the sudden quiet under the trees, with the light on the water glimmering up through the turning foliage, they were frightened. They told him they really needed to get to New Haven and he replied, *Yeah, but we were going to get high.* The girls said that maybe they shouldn't. The man was quiet again, Eve said. He glared at the water as if the view hurt his feelings and said, *Did you ever see anything so beautiful?* My sister said that they looked at the water but did not find it beautiful. Then he raised his voice. *Well, how about that song, anyway, before we get going?* he said, and they were relieved and said they wanted to hear it. *My ax is in the trunk,* he said, and they all got out and walked around to the back of the car. He opened the trunk and reached inside, and when he straightened up again, Eve said, he was holding a tire iron. And then his arm as if spring-loaded flicked toward her, the impact of the bar crushing the bones on the left side of her face and the bridge of her nose and driving a splinter of bone into her eye.

When she regained consciousness, she was alone in the dark. She tried to stand up, but the pain kept her down, and she passed out again. When she came to, the woods were full of light and the singing of birds. She crawled to the road, where she was picked up by a man and a boy who were on their way to fish the reservoir.

Peggy's body was discovered a month later in a ditch in Hartford.

The big console stereo in the living room had always belonged, more or less, to Michele and me, but after Peggy was killed, the parents took it back. They buried our records under a mound of their own—old, heavy 33s that slid out of their sleeves with authority, and even a few 78s, glossy, hazed with age, filled with jumpy music that clawed the air. Dad built manhattans while Mom bent her face to the labels. Swimming in her dress, worn down to the thinness of the handle of a pitchfork plunged into the heart of grief, she looked as though she would will into being the mood she would suffer. Then she and Father drifted together and clung, through long afternoons that floated on smooth music and the swish and rustle of Mother's dress. The Chief, steeped in bourbon—even his new paleness seemed to mellow to the rusty color of booze—anchored himself swayingly in the middle of the floor and spun his partner through the odd and fancy figures of dances they'd learned back when they first met. They went through the military motions of a tango and tried the rush and whirl of a waltz but settled finally on the rhumba, that simple movable rectangle, spinning their grief in a slowly spiraling *pietà* in which the living hold and comfort the living.

≈

I returned to San Diego three weeks later and let myself into the apartment. Leo had kept the place neat, as always, right to the penciled note, squared to the edge of the kitchen table. I slipped it from beneath a seashell.

I am very sorry but received word this week of immediate transfer and have had to move as quickly as you might imagine. I wish you well, never otherwise. D.

≈

I have noticed lately that all my memories now have equal weight. A sea change of middle age? Some rearrangement of the ballast between my ears? It's a small thing, but to discover that the world of my memory no longer discriminates between the recent past—this morning, or ten minutes ago—and the past of a world so distant it might be hiding on the other side of the stars, while no great shock, is still a sadness. It was not so long ago that I also noticed, climbing a staircase in strong morning light, that the skin of my arms was covered with dust. But looking more closely, I saw that what I had thought dust was instead a fine, soft skein of wrinkles. So the past, loosened from the net of memory, swims away, while I am held more firmly than ever here, in what appears to be the present.

I refuse to do billboards, or even to sell them. I ask my customers, Why pollute a world of any size? *Yes,* they say, lifting one of Michele's creations out of the box, *but it's not the real world.* No, I say. It is not. All the more reason to leave it alone.

Fired from the service, I came home to Darien to find the household breaking up. Michele had come close to getting her degree, but left school when Peggy was killed, waffled about going back, then didn't, then went to work for a graphic designer. Dad found a buyer for the house. He took the couple through the building, top to bottom, throwing open doors, thumping walls, demonstrating the soundness of every switch, latch, and appliance, right down to the basement, where the papers lay on the bar, waiting to be signed.

Everyone but Eve was glad to go. Michele took Mrs. Claus and got an apartment in town, above Ackerman's Hardware, and I slid in there with her temporarily, sleeping on the couch, playing with the cat—but gingerly, now. Stroking the whitening throat she turned up to my touch. I hung out in my alien civvies, lonely, bruised inside.

Mother and Dad moved to a condo village—one of the first of these—on the other side of town. "Miller's Creek," both mill and creek having been obliterated in the process of its creation. They settled in just before Thanksgiving, and on the day, Michele and I went over together. "Don't laugh," Dad said when he opened the door. "It was a great deal." Theirs was the model unit.

At dinner—our first Thanksgiving with an empty chair—we couldn't get the rhythm right. The Chief shrugged, talked, kept the conversation going. He was skinnier, but no less quick; sharper, if anything, as if he sensed dullness in the air and would cut it free, but the smudges under his eyes were the size of thumbprints, his skin sallow as a poor man's candle. He lamented the end of the business, but without fuss. "No one wants small anymore," he said, and pointed at the TV. "Unless it's that."

But occasionally a client appeared. Dad took me into the apartment's little den and rattled out a rolled-up drawing. A church. Two hundred years. A Celebration of Our Heritage. Dad grimaced. "Your mother doesn't think much of it. Neither do I, tell the truth. I'll put it this way: It's goddamned dull." But his fingers caressed the picture's solemn lines. He let go of the drawing and it rolled itself up.

"Tell you what, John. I'd like to do it, anyway. Just for fun. Of course, we don't have a shop. What can you do without a shop?"

He glanced around the box-like room. Walls and ceiling smooth as sheets of paper, rectilinear windows, their sills bland as balsa wood, the glass flawless, spotless. The carpet beneath our feet soft as felt you'd slash with a razor just to see it fall away from the blade.

I smoothed the drawing open, grabbed books, dealt them to the corners to hold the paper flat. Mother came in, Eve at her elbow. They were seldom apart.

"Oh, dear," Mother said. "This thing." But she, too, touched the drawing. We all looked down at the artist's work. Eve's fingers traced the irises sketched beneath the building's bank of windows. "Pretty," she said, and gave her hand to Mother. But the flowers, the tall casements designed to drink sunlight, the white exterior—the whiteness of a purity we believe we can turn to—said to us only that Peggy had gone out of the world.

Nevertheless, we looked down at the drawing as if we were seeing our own home, all together, for the first time. Because just then, Michele came in. Finding ourselves in a circle around the table, we joined hands.

And looking over at Mother's face, I remembered again who she was.

This is what I mean:

When Mom and Dad took that little vacation—the only one, I think, that they've ever taken—and returned home, their problems apparently mended, I registered a shock: I didn't know my mother. After Dad came in, in the slow seconds of the screen door's drifting back, I had spied Mom sitting in the car—and in the moment before she looked up and pulled her face into a smile for Michele, who'd run out to greet her, I didn't recognize her.

In those seconds, what I saw was just a woman sitting in a car, like any number of women I'd seen in parking lots and in the street and in stores—anonymous, bearing lives I'd never given a moment's thought to except to classify and catalog as members of what I called the female race: girls, wives, women, sisters, mothers. Peering into purses and mirrors, scanning shelves, looking for change or cold remedies or reaching for a baby or prodding a sulky toddler. Women of the world—or of no world I knew existed. *Their* world, it is theirs. The small world that sits within and completes other worlds: the little world of oil and gears and heartbeats and joys and vanishings and the silences of the everyday and the every night. The world we keep breaking down and they keep building and giving back and back and back into our hands.

White

Without thinking, she hit him. And because she had not made a fist—for all that had been said, she had not expected to strike her husband—Sheila's blow was neither slap nor punch, but a flail of nail-tipped fingers that zipped open the skin under his near-side eye. The cigarette he had just put to his lips flicked itself neatly out the driver's-side window as his hands shot up in a reflex of shock, and as she pushed the door open, she thought: *He doesn't know what hit him.*

They'd just seen a baseball game. Grant had played in high school and college, but out of school for seven years, he liked to watch, now. Televised games, mostly, but sometimes, like today, the Padres, high up beneath the blazing sun.

They drank beer. Excited, Grant scratched his tingling buzz-cut scalp, pointed down through acres of broiling air, detailing the players' mistakes, while Sheila nodded.

Afterward, disoriented in the crowds churning through the exits, Sheila lost him. When at last she found the car, she slipped in and buckled up, smoothed black hair down the nape of her neck, didn't look at him. Didn't have to.

"Look," he said, tuning the AC. "I told you I wanted to get out of here fast." Also trying to back the car into a break that closed as suddenly as it had opened. "Now look."

"I was trying to hurry. I couldn't keep up with you. We didn't even see all of the last inning."

"We know how it *ends*, Sheila. Well, now we're stuck." Grant lay on the horn but no one seemed to notice.

Sheila's voice notched up into the harsh, defeated range. "Well, I can't keep up with you," she said. "I don't like walking alone."

She gazed out at the acres of cars and thought of the television westerns she'd watched growing up back East: plains alive with restive, murmuring cattle, rain sifting from Technicolor skies. They were sitting not more than ten miles from their neighborhood's strip malls and lock-step streets, rows of pastel-bright houses with low-pitched, pebbled roofs, west-facing bedroom windows sealed from the sun with aluminum foil. With the AC on, the car had rapidly cooled. Everything she had loved about California had already evaporated off her skin. And now this.

"If I wanted to walk alone, I'd go for a walk by myself."

"Well, *go ahead*, for Christ's sake." The hands that gripped the wheel fell to his sides. "We have plenty of time now."

Sheila stared at him. "Would you like me to?"

His eyes rested on hers for the first time that day. "Whatever. Whatever you want."

She sprung the catch and the seat belt slithered aside. "Okay," she said. "I'm going." She opened the door.

"*Oh*, boy—oh yeah" he said, and reached automatically for his cigarettes. "Weird City. Here it comes." He put a cigarette between his lips.

Without thinking, Sheila hit him.

≈

In the grocery store, Sheila would watch as Grant rounded the end of an aisle, disappearing into, say, Dairy. She'd catch up in, say, Wine & Beer. He'd be putting a six-pack into the cart: "What—you want to spend the night here?"

When they attended church, Grant rose with the choir for the closing hymn and bolted, leaving her to stand in the queue to speak to the minister.

They had recently attended the funeral of Sheila's aunt. As Sheila contemplated the finality of a quarter ton of earth heaped next to a hole in the ground, Grant, beside her, said, "Okay?" That night in their hotel, Grant preceded her in sleep. Sheila lay awake, viewing in her mind's eye an image of the distance between Grant and herself until the picture—a kind of weepy seascape—dissolved in a white light that was like sleep, and then was sleep.

~

Grant recovered, grabbed at her, caught the neck of her T-shirt. Sheila fought not to fall, then went with the overbalance, throwing her arms up and back. She knocked the mirror askew; her other hand struck Grant. Fearing another attack, he flinched—and Sheila slid down and out, leaving him holding the empty top. In a moment she was sprawled on the pavement. She scrambled up and walked quickly away from the car.

Breathing was hard, walking was hard. The air she sucked in got tangled in the dry cloth of her throat. Her legs twitched her along like panicky animals on leads. Straight ahead but blocks away rose the trestles of traffic lights and signs. Beyond them, elevated, cars flashed by on the highway. Sheila turned aside.

A lick of pain ran up the knuckles of her spine to where her bra clasped. She thought of going back—the skin of her bare shoulders and belly prickled as if chilled, not heated by exposure—but didn't. She made her way through the personal spaces the shifting cars required, lightly touching the hot hoods and trunks as if they were tumbled boulders along a path she wished to remember and would later retrace.

~

The noise of the AC and the radio racket were enough to block out the sound of laughter Grant had heard from the car next to his— laughter he knew was directed at him. Lost-his-wife-in-a-parking-lot laughter. But they were gone now, and Sheila was out there in her bra and shorts. He flicked the fan down a notch and something snappy breezed from the cream-colored recessed speaker screens. Sheila's T-shirt lay on the seat as if she had casually dropped it there, and he took it in his fingers to feel the shapeless innocence of cloth without a body. Then he put his face into the shirt to get the scent of her.

~

Sheila crossed a rectangle of browned grass, then walked along the perimeter fence until she came to a rip. Pressing aside the broken fingers of wire, she pushed through to a discarded lot of scabbed asphalt empty of all but a single car parked near the fence in a patch of shade. A young man got out of the car. He held up a can of beer as if he were about to endorse it and said, "Hey." Three other boys were sitting one-two-three, pupils on a bench, all laughing, in the car's back seat. In the passenger seat, a young woman with red hair knotted at her crown to fountain up and then spill over, brushed the falling hair aside to see Sheila better. Her mouth opened.

≈

There was an afternoon—a year ago, when he and Sheila had been fixing dinner together, drinking Mexican beer and laughing about something. They were both high from the day, the beer—whatever. He had kissed the nape of her neck while she was slicing peppers— the little kisses she liked. The knife clattered into the sink as she turned in his arms. She took his hand and led him to the bedroom, and then she flicked this same T-shirt over her head and let it fall. *I was sitting on the bed.* Waiting for whatever she wanted, wanting to do nothing but what she wanted. *She moved between my legs* and put her hands, still wet and cool from the vegetables, on the back of his head and pressed *her fingers against my neck and pulled my face to her breasts.*

≈

"Hey, dolly." The driver of the car smiled at Sheila. "Do you want a ride or anything?" He gestured toward the car as if to say, My chariot awaits. His reversed ball cap, fitted to the eyebrows, produced a bleakly humorous impression of retardation. The boys in the back seat laughed again and shouted. The female passenger took her eyes off Sheila and reached over the seat and slapped at the boys, who held up their hands and laughed harder. "Let me out! Out! Let me the fuck out!" One by one they shouted.

Sheila walked to the car and took the can of beer from the boy. The little that was left tasted vile, was sulphurously warm, but soaking. A boy de-cocooned through a window, came up behind Shei-

la and put his hands around her middle. "Is that good?" he asked.
"Yes," the driver said. "It's great." Sheila pulled the boy's fingers from
her skin and the hands, as if released from gravity, floated. "Okay,"
he said, but the hands, contrite and duplicitous, settled again on
her bare stomach.

"Wild baby," the driver said. "Baby doll, *baby*, I bet your titties
are fine."

The three kids still in the car had all gotten out. The female passenger lit a cigarette, leaned her lower arms on the car's roof and
instantly flinched back. "Hoo!—hot!"

Sheila felt hands on her ass and a mumble of fingers along the
waistband of her shorts. The rapt, attentive boys moved with her
when she moved and she moved with the slow sliding of their bodies through the chutes of a bloodless slaughterhouse. She pushed
against them, felt the partitions of muscle and bone relent, give
way, reassert. They were at her as at a window, looking in where she
boiled like a kettle of snow, where she looked out at something she
had once wanted, something planted in her as deeply as a tongue is
rooted in the dark. One boy's suppressed erection was against her
thigh like a knot. Another boy's hands cupped her breasts. *This is
my body.*

The driver pumped his hands in a cop's slow-down gesture and
said, "Let's get dolly into the car."

Grant watched the miniature traffic surge through the heat rolling
up off the access road. The main lot was deserted but for two or
three dingy cars, each sitting alone, as if someone had wanted to
prevent them influencing one another.

His face was no longer bleeding. He had looked in the rearview
mirror once after Sheila left and now he looked again. Just scratch-
es, really, but eager bleeders all the same. Seeing them scared the
shit out of him.

She'd got him—no mistake.

He lay his hand on the slope of the dashboard—nothing like the
metal dashboards in his father's cars, the kind kids dashed their

brains out on back before some genius figured out that bodies continue to move forward when a car slams to a stop. Was restraint such a hard lesson to learn?

"I don't have time for this," he said. "I don't have time for this or any other lesson. I can't wait any longer."

"Not in *my* car," the fountain-haired girl said. She glared at the driver, who opened his arms wide as if to say, You're crucifying me.

The boys ceased stroking Sheila. They waited. A boy said, "Aw, *man.*" The girl flicked her lips tenderly with a tendril of red hair and regarded Sheila. "Why don't you take a walk, chick, unless you just *want* to get fucked."

Sheila considered. Did she *want* to get fucked by four boys in the back seat of a car? Hadn't she seen that happen in a movie? A queue of men at the open back door of a car and a man inside, pumping away between a woman's legs, his romping white ass—that which is always behind us—absurdly comical? *Last Exit to Brooklyn.* Nearly the last scene. The woman had pulled off her blouse in a bar in a gesture of drunken defiance or madness that ignited the room's haze of latent carnality. She pulled the white blouse open and screamed, *"Take a look at these!"* and the men swamped her. In the next shot, she was on her back and the men were lined up. Quiet, like now—sober, you could say. Solid. Ready. Waiting for a turn.

Why had she done it? What did she want?

"I have to go, now," Sheila said.

The driver touched Sheila's jaw, let his fingers slide to her lips. Sheila opened her mouth, sucked in an inch of his sticky fuck-you finger, and bit it to the bone. The boy screamed. The other boys fell away from her, and she ran away.

"*And* talking to yourself again," he said. "That's fucked up, Grant. That's what crazy people do. I've seen them—everybody has. Do they ever shut up? In their rooms, or wherever they live, do they ever quiet down and just . . ." Grant put his hands on the wheel, rocked it slightly back and forth. "And just sit there, think about things, make phone calls? Do their wives run off in a parking lot in the middle of the motherfucking day?"

There was no one left in the parking lot. He was the last. "No, they don't," he said. "Those people don't have wives."

"I'm the last one," he said. "I'm the last person out here."

≈

The houses in the neighborhood beyond the shadow of the ball-park were dingy, sun-bleached with age, and small. Sheila knocked at the door of the first house she came to, waited, then jogged to the next one, then the next. *It's California, no one's home.* At the fourth house a woman peered at Sheila through a small pane of yellow-tinted glass and withdrew. The door opened.

"Yes? What is it?" Her speech had a drowsy southern dip. A heavy woman, past middle age. Sheila realized, irrelevantly, that she didn't know which years were supposed to define middle age now. The woman looked old to her—looked her mother's age—with that generation's comforting roundness, its Depression-era quality of having been irrevocably shaped to please and fated to serve.

"Yes?"

"I need a shirt or something. Even a T-shirt. Please."

After a moment, the woman stepped back and Sheila walked in. A table lamp burned intensely—*a yellow hole in the gray air so I know it's not dark, it's my eyes.* The languid air she had felt flowing around her ankles at the door now enveloped and calmed her. The house was blissfully cool. When the woman shut the door, Sheila heard, in the cessation of the freeway noise, the rustle of an air conditioner. Her whole situation suddenly became clear to her. The penny-bitter taste of the boy driver's beer and blood, the seared white skin of her shoulders. "My husband's waiting for me," she said, and turning to the woman, she blundered into her arms and wept loudly.

≈

Grant lit a cigarette and smoked it hard, letting the smoke fill up the car. In his mind, he was sitting in a room, talking to himself. "That'll be the day," he said out loud. "That will be the fucking day, boy."

But still, the room was in a city, and this had to be faced. An eastern or midwestern city, New York or Cleveland, Detroit, someplace dark—yes? Winter. Burned-out urban arroyos, where the pores of the living exhaled poverty and ruin into air that poured it back into their lungs. There were rich people and middle-class people in those cities, too, but he didn't know them. His people, the room people, were the ones he knew. Every time he slowed down, they were there, waiting. They were not evil or repulsive, but they were inevitable, they were *his people*, and that was far worse.

"My people." Grant dumped Sheila's purse upside down on the seat. Sunlight riffled the keys and plastic surfaces of her things. Lighter things fell and bounced: a pencil, a little book, matches, a comb. A whiff of sulphur from the matchbook, the greasy sweetness of a lipstick when he held it to his nose. Tissues, some bearing lip-prints. A tube of eyeliner. "She loves her beauty stuff," he said. "You really love your beauty stuff, don't you?"

He opened the little book. On its cover: *Memo*. Notes to herself. Shopping. Things that she needed to do. Scribbles, then some twenty blank pages at the end.

Grant flipped through them. Empty.

Days that had not yet happened—these would need notes, direction, reason.

Blanks. Starting today.

Waiting for a mark, a sign. Empty.

White.

God damn it. God damn it.

~

The woman, whose name was Eleanor, brought her rattletrap car to a stop in front of Grant and Sheila's house. Sheila was wearing one of Eleanor's blouses, and in spite of the heat she felt cool inside the older woman's large size.

Eleanor had brought out the blouse for Sheila, then taken her to the bathroom to clean and dress her back. She gave her glasses of water. She insisted on taking her home—if she wanted to go home.

"I do." Sheila let her head drop forward and pressed her eyes into the heels of her hands. They were sitting in Eleanor's kitchen. Eleanor's husband had come home and been intercepted, then dispatched to another part of the house.

"You're welcome to stay till you're sure."

"I'm sure—I guess I am. Oh, *shit*, I don't know what I am." She had told Eleanor about everything except the boys.

"I'll give you my number—here." Eleanor pulled the note from the pad. "You can just call me, any time, you know. Doesn't have to be for a special reason."

Now Sheila got out of the car and looked back in and thanked Eleanor again and said, "Okay, then"—she felt she'd put on Eleanor's lazy dialect as well—"Well, I *will* call you."

"You should!"

"I love this shirt," Sheila said, and blushed to feel such unashamed love.

≈

Grant swept the keys and cosmetics violently off the seat. A small object ricocheted, striking him in the face, and he vaulted out of the car, slamming the door so hard that something came loose inside it and fell, tinkling. He kicked the door to ensure that it was really shut, really broken—and to break it further, to fuck it up.

Then he tried to open the door—but it wouldn't open. He went around to the passenger side and found that one locked.

"Well, you are really and truly screwed now, boy" he said. The car idled complacently.

Grant began to kick the car, which remained sealed. He jogged over to one of the deserted cars, set himself, kicked off its driver's side mirror, and took it back to his car. He was winding up to smash the mirror through the window when something moved in the periphery of his vision. He turned his head.

Two policemen were getting out of their vehicle. One had a service pistol in his hand. The other held up a hand in warning. "Don't move, sir," he said, "just stand right there and be real, real still, nice and still and nice, and quiet," the men moving away from the patrol car now and coming together and then letting their paths diverge as they walked toward Grant, whose thoughts simply seized up as he understood that the worst had truly happened. He could rest now because—well, not only *am I about to be shot for breaking into my own car?* but—things were so simple, really. When they unraveled and unwound and broke and fell apart *and stopped moving and cracked open*, things became understandable. No—bearable. Bearable, and *unbearably whole in my broken, fucked-up-ness.* They caught up with you, and then they had you, and they put you in a room. And then you could never get away.

Sheila walked up the driveway and around to the back of the house and found the key they kept hidden where no one but a burglar would find it. She let herself in and walked unhurriedly through the house to the bedroom to pick up the telephone she had heard ringing when she opened the back door.

"Sheila?"

Grant! She could hear background noises but couldn't make out if they were bar noises or what.

"Sheila? It's me. I'm—Sheila, I'm in jail."

Sheila waited.

"Are you there?"

"I'm here."

"I'm being held. I'm at—" His voice became small and went, *Where am I?* He came back. "I'm in custody. Downtown."

The background noise of telephones, voices, a man's deep laughter, chatter, suggested a happy day at the station—inconsequence came down the line. There was Grant's breathing, then sipping sounds. *He is in jail and having a cup of coffee.* She liked the idea of his being detained—and it occurred to her that she might remember the last time she had liked *him*: who he was, his ideas, his terrible manners, his bad dreams, the way his bare legs felt against hers, his urgency, his sudden shrinking. The way he could talk to a child in a natural way but not want one of his own. Of their own. His refusal to wear sunblock, her beating on his locked heart. His wanting to get ahead. His fear of falling behind. Her fear of falling with him.

"I'll call you back," she said, and hung up.

She walked through the house, turning on lights, then searched the back of a drawer that concealed her stash of cigarettes—she had "quit" months ago and had been sneaking them for months. She made coffee and took a cup into the bedroom and sat on the bed and smoked the cigarette and drank coffee, then lit another cigarette and lay back and smoked it.

Sheila picked up the telephone and punched in numbers.

"Hello," she said. "Eleanor?"

When Sheila arrived at the police station she found Grant sitting, not in a cell, but on a plastic chair in a room. She could not catch his eye as she approached because he was leaning forward, face to the floor, elbows in his thighs. She took the chair next to his.

"Hey," she said. She didn't touch him because she was afraid that, if she did, he would not say what he might've been about to say— a touch could throw a man off the beam—and she wanted to hear whatever he might say, more than she wanted to touch him.

Grant wiped his face with his hands in long, slow strokes, as if washing.

"When you hung up, I was afraid you might not come. I mean, they told me I could go, you know, they don't even know who owns the car I *vandalized*, they just think I'm out of my fucking mind. But I had to get in touch with you first and make sure it was all right. I mean"—and now he looked up at her and she saw the bandage under his eye—"I know it isn't *all right*. Nothing is all right. I've got to go up in front of a judge. I broke—"

Abruptly he raised his head. Face clenched like a fist. "I broke the law. I broke a mirror off somebody's car. The car—our car— was running but I was locked out and I wanted to get back in and then the cops came and pulled a gun on me, a fucking *gun*, Sheila. Oh, *God*."

He cried briefly in a sound so primitive it seemed to issue not from his throat but to be claw-hammered out of his chest, nails out of old clapboards, and she thought, *Why do they hold it in till it's this bad?*

"They impounded the car." After crying, his voice was raw. "I locked myself out of the car, Sheila. *That* was stupid."

"I had a cigarette," she said.

"What? I know. I mean—I didn't know *today*. I found them, so I knew. I was looking for something and—well, surprise. I didn't know whether to say anything or not. I wanted to say something."

"It was wonderful," she said.

Grant looked at her and his face clenched again, but he did not yield. "Oh, yeah? That's great. I mean, I guess it is. I guess I don't know what to make of it. We were going to quit together, weren't we?"

Sheila took his wounded face in her hands.

"Let's do that."

"Sheila, I don't know what to make of it. I don't know where the hell I'm going," he said. "I know I'm going, but I don't know where."

"You can go with me," she replied. "I have a car waiting."

House of Prayer

When I hear the last of Joellen's people leaving—when the singing stops—I take off my headphones and go down to the kitchen. Joellen is putting some glasses into the sink; she hums a gospel tune as she squeezes a stream of dish soap into the hot water, and sweet, scalded citrus perfumes the air. Her steel-string guitar leans against the table, an upright lady with hard, lacquered hips. When I scratch my fingernails across the strings, Joellen turns to me and smiles.

Joellen always looks sleepy and elated after one of her meetings. I take this as proof of a great burden—or, at least, an overabundance—of a kind of happiness I simply don't understand. I have seen other faces stirred by the distress of a single, powerful emotion and one, closer to home, by the toxins of insanity. But Joellen's face is transformed—made radiant—by nothing more complicated than the presence of divine love.

"Beth," she says. "I hope you weren't disturbed. It was a good one tonight."

"I wasn't disturbed."

Joellen nods. She retrieves glasses, swabs them with a dishcloth and sets them in rows on the drainboard.

"You should join us some night. If you want to, I mean. You're invited."

"Oh I know!" I say, hating the bright tone I use with her. "Maybe I will."

But I know I won't.

It's not just because I don't believe—I struggle, at difficult moments in my life, to believe in *something*—but because, unlike Joellen, I'm not saved. Though lost, I don't feel I'm even a candidate for search and rescue. Keeping my own counsel (and counseling myself rarely), my idea of heaven, when I look up, is a fall sky pierced by a wavering arrow of Canada geese, making their way in a clamor of intuitive wisdom. They, at least, always seem to know where they're going.

But then, so does she.

I met Joellen when I answered her ad requesting a roommate. I'd moved in with a stranger once before—a woman in her twenties, same as me—but hadn't liked it: she was a complete slob and there wasn't enough privacy, besides. So I was relieved when Joellen walked me through her spacious apartment in the big turn-of-the-century house. She took me upstairs, showing me a long, carpeted hallway, a bathroom, and the two bedrooms. There was a little room at the end of the hall Joellen used, she said, for sewing and knitting and for "less temporal" kinds of contemplation.

"Really?" I asked, interested. "Like TM?"

I had tried meditation: By night, mantric syllables floated through a revolving door in my mind. But eventually I gave it up (as I give up most things), preferring to let my thoughts drift, unblocked and unaltered, toward oblivion.

Joellen smiled. She lifted a loop of golden hair away from her face and I was embarrassed, suddenly: I'd apparently asked something personal. Then I got a feeling—a premonition.

"Meditation, sure—and prayer. Do you pray?" she said.

"Well, not really," I replied, thinking *Oh, God.* "Not if you mean *pray* pray." She continued to smile at me, and I made a business of looking around the room. The little there was to see—white, unadorned walls, high ceiling, one small gothic window tucked into the eave—confirmed the fleeting impression I had had upon entering: this was a nun's room. A cell.

Back downstairs, Joellen faced me with folded arms. "I'm born again," she said. "Not a church lady, though." Grinning, guiding me to the door: "It's not a requirement and I don't proselytize. But think about it. Call me when you've made your decision."

As I walked to my car I felt certain—a certainty born out of envy of whatever appears to be certain in others—that as a maker of decisions, Joellen had it all over me: what to embrace, how to live; things I couldn't get my arms around. I settled myself into the cold car, feeling a bitter affinity with the iron-cold steering wheel, the dim windows, the engine that hung onto its cold-weather crankiness all year.

But—after an hour and a half at home, I called Joellen and told her I'd be glad to move in as soon as possible.

～

Joellen's friend Julian is over. Joellen is chopping celery and carrots for stock. I've already cracked the chicken bones and got them boiling and Julian's sitting at the kitchen table, strumming his guitar. He's working on a new song about Jesus—not the watchful Jesus I encountered in catechism classes at Saint Theresa's but a strangely unambitious Christ with an exposed, burning heart; a Jesus who, in Julian's phrases, *waits, ever patient*, at the threshold of a closed door.

Julian doesn't talk about the life he led before being saved, but his face, spoon-narrow and sandblast-clean of what must have been a plague of acne, looks a perfect portrait of dissolution purified. And his voice, as if to compensate for a backslider's mumbles, hits you with an evangelist's lung-power: a nearly white mustache bristles in the wind of his zeal.

"I'm real pleased to meet you," he shouted when we were introduced. "Real, *real* pleased." He held my arms just above the elbows and sort of shook me, as if expecting fruit to fall from my upper branches. After that, I'd try to arrange it so that we said hello from across the room.

Joellen found this strategy transparent—and amusing. "Julian's a wild man," she said between gulps of laughter. "The boy's a pea-picker."

In truth, I was annoyed Joellen had noticed my jitters: I'd been threading my way through her friends as I would have worked the shallow, muddy waters of a pond in my bare feet, poised to leap away from any touch of clinging Christian passion. But while I appreciated their respectful distance and charitable smiles (on behalf of my smudged soul?), I also felt a puzzling—and paradoxical—disappointment at feeling left out. I noticed how they were with one another: unironical, genuinely cool, gentle. So—didn't I count? Wasn't I the perfect candidate for some of this love, despite my armor?

"Of course you count," Joellen says. We've moved upstairs and are sitting in opposite corners of the couch beneath the gothic window in what I've begun to call (to myself) the Last Supper Club. Joellen's knitting is in her lap. Downstairs, Julian struggles with his song, his skinny voice as abrasive as the smell of simmering stock.

"Of *course* you count. But people don't expect you to be someone else. You're you." Joellen shrugs to show me how simple this is. "You're Beth." She reaches over and takes my hands in hers and I flush like a child; I register a child's mixed feelings of pleasure and alarm at being *seized*.

"I know," I say, lamely. I lower my eyes but feel Joellen's on my face like a light.

Joellen pulls another heap of wheat-colored wool from her bag and resumes knitting. My hands, left to their own devices, are idle, so I weave the fingers into a knot, take a breath, and begin to tell her about my sister, Lauren.

This is the story I tell:

Lauren's three years younger than I am and lives at home. She sleeps (we think) between two and four hours a night and spends her days pacing the house, smoking, and ranting. If she comes to the dinner table at all, she brings a book and reads instead of eating. She seems to live mostly on snacks. Medication keeps her semi-normal, but she'll never be *right*.

"Never right—if you want to put it that way," one of her first doctors told us. "But manageable, certainly." My mother and father and I were sitting in his office at Mercy Hospital. Lauren was incarcerated, at that time, in a distant wing of the building.

Lauren had been unmanageable, more or less, since she was fifteen. It began with prolonged fits of weeping followed by week-long silences, and nightmares from which she seemed unable to fully awaken. In photographs, she seems to shrink toward the edge of the frame, her face raw with fear, alert to a kind of suffering the camera cannot help but catch.

"Well, for God's sweet sake," my father said. "Manageable? What the hell does that mean? She's only just turned seventeen."

Mother sat quietly, hands folded, her gaze resting lightly on the doctor—no doubt, erasing him. She would hire another doctor. Then another.

"I wish I had better news," the doctor said. "I really do. But schizophrenia tends to deepen." He frowned. "I can give you that she'll have periods of lucidity, but it's in the nature of this disease, in the long run, to be unpredictable, and degenerative."

(Lauren's nonstop talking, her rages, her disappearing act after she's spit her pills into the trash for a few days running: very unpredictable. Her long, one-sided conversations with Jimi Hendrix: very deep.)

But Lauren does indeed have her lucid moments—lucid but skewed, full of random sharpness.

One morning when I was still living at home, Lauren came into my bedroom carrying two mugs of tea. Placing these on the bedside table, she flipped on the light. I don't usually get up at five but I struggled to sit up, accepted the mug of tea Lauren thrust at me, and waited while she smoothed the sheets and rearranged the blanket over my knees. I couldn't see her eyes—Lauren always wears shades—but a smear of dark flesh showed beneath the black rim of each lens: two half-moons in negative, proof of my sister's enforced vigilance, the stamp of her virtual sleeplessness.

And then she did something that splashed me like a spray of sleet: she smiled—the smile that I had nearly forgotten, and missed, and which squeezed my heart now, painfully.

"Hydroponics," Lauren said. "I've been thinking about it all night. You can grow things without putting them into the ground. Think of it!" She drank some of her tea, fumbled a cigarette out of the pocket of her robe, and lit up. "*Think* of it."

"Sounds good," I said.

"Sounds good to you *now*, but who knows how you'll feel about it later?" The smile was gone. "In six weeks, when summer is here, how will you feel then? I know plants belong to the earth. Is it wrong to subvert nature, or so common that we simply don't see it? I won't always be able to live here, not after Mom and Dad are dead. This house is so small." Lauren stared into her cup, drew it close, and puffed a little smoke into it, thickening the luxuriant steam. "I'm going to grow vegetables hydroponically and live off them. I'm not going to kill any more animals. I *refuse*—"

She looked toward the still-darkened window and moved her head slowly from side to side; too slowly for wonder, too slowly, almost, to signal a negation.

"I'm so worried," she whispered.

"What about, baby?"

"Oh, vegetables and fruits. How the space keeps changing in this house, stuff like that." She took a deep drag and dropped the half-smoked cigarette into her cup. "My room's just about ready for hydroponic gardening. If I had more windows, more sunlight, I'd be set. I'd never have to leave the house. I wouldn't have to worry about dirt or drought or root suffocation. But it's wrong."

"What is, Laurie?" I took a sip of Lauren's bitter tea and braced myself for the ride.

"The *roots*. The *prairie*. They're living creatures, you know. There's no difference in things. Like in Kafka's story: it wasn't revulsion or piety or even purity, it was that the hunger artist couldn't find what he *liked to eat*. Think of that. If he had, he would've stuffed himself. And the pictures I've seen—you can see everything: in hydroponics, the roots hang down in the water, floating like tentacles, they glisten like intestines. Nothing is hidden. You think it is, but it isn't. It can't ever be. That's where we're wrong. That's where the hunger artist was *wrong*."

I felt myself pulling away from her craziness. Perfectly natural—but there was a stain on it, a smear of infidelity.

"Laurie," I said. "Baby. It's okay. I'll always be here even if—"

Lauren put her fingers over my lips.

"Listen to me," she said. "Nothing is hidden forever. Hiding means disappearing and then reappearing, an inside-out thing. You think it's difference, and *growth*, but it isn't. *It's all one thing.* And one day you look in the mirror and don't know who the hell you are. Trust me."

Lauren stood up, smoothed the place where she'd been sitting and collected the cups. "Or don't," she said. In a few minutes I heard her running the water for the first of her half dozen daily showers.

I finish my story. Joellen has added two inches to the arm of the sweater she's knitting, and now she lets her hands drop into her lap. "Lord," she says, and looks at me. "You will hate me for what I am going to say."

"No! I wouldn't—"

"Beth, it's all for the good."

I am lost, and I say so.

"Everything that happens—even the bad things, maybe even especially the senseless, evil things—they're for the good."

≈

I told my boyfriend, Hank, that I was feeling unsure about where our relationship was going; and I hedged by adding that I needed some time to figure that out, when in reality I didn't really need any time—I knew it was all but over. We'd met on a blind date and after two months I felt we were going nowhere special. Not that I blamed him; he hadn't been any more particular than I had. But I would have liked it if he'd wanted me more—or wanted more of me, and been willing to dig for it. The fact that he didn't, that we seemed rapidly to be approaching the status of people who smile and nod and move on when they meet in the supermarket—that made me so sad. To save my own feelings, I turned it on him.

Hank looked mournful. "It's my fault," he said. "I know it is."

"*No*," I said. "It's no one's fault. Really."

"You're mad, aren't you?"

I waited to speak until the surge of guilty anger had passed. "No," I said. "But, Hank, I'm going to get mad pretty soon."

He nodded. "I knew it."

We were sitting in his truck in the parking lot of a hill-town cowboy bar called the Ranch Hand. Every time the door opened, smoke and noise spewed into the night. Two men stumbled out now and wandered to the side of the building. They unzipped, then pissed against the Ranch Hand's yellow-painted cinderblock. One of the men rested his forehead against the wall and groaned while the other laughed and sang along with the music that thumped through the wall.

Hank said, "Those guys could use the john. They don't have to come out here."

"They probably just like the wide-open spaces," I said, feeling unreasonably cross. "Where the buffalo roam and all that."

"You really are mad, aren't you?"

"Maybe I *am*. Maybe you should just take me home."

Which is what I wish I'd said the week before.

On that night, we'd stayed at the bar until eleven o'clock, then driven—both of us more than a little drunk—over to Sawmill Falls. The falls begin as a noisy stream that widens as it runs steeply downhill through the woods. There's a pool at the site of the old sawmill, about halfway to the bottom. With the fluid confidence of the inebriated, I ran ahead of Hank and found the place.

A tremendous, frightful torrent of water lashed through the trees, white in the moonlight, but the pool itself was a deep, dark, open eye. Kicking off my boots, leaving my clothes where they dropped, I leaped into space, pulling my knees tight against my breasts at the last moment and cannonballing into the water.

An ice-blade of sobriety sliced through the alcohol as I dropped

"Hell, that's all right," Hank said, and turned around.

Which is when I placed my hands on his chest and pushed him into the water.

I finish browning hamburger and onions and pour canned tomatoes and beans over them, then add chili powder, ground cumin, red pepper. The sound of guitars drifts down from upstairs; Joellen's and Julian's voices penetrate the Last Supper Club's closed door: a fervent and painful harmony.

"They're pretty bad," Hank says from his seat at the table. He smiles, looking hangdog, and I know he thinks it'd be nice if I agreed. But I don't; in fact, I surprise myself by taking offense at his remark: what business is it of his?

And why am I cooking dinner for this guy?

Ever since I nearly drowned Hank at the falls—I did not know he couldn't swim, and in fact I had to jump in and pull him out—I've been trying, unsuccessfully, to close him out of my life in less lethal ways. At the moment, though, he's stuck to my hull like a barnacle.

Joellen walks into the kitchen holding an empty glass in each hand.

"*Something* smells wonderful. Hello, Hank, what's new?"

Considerable shuffling from Hank's corner. I smile into the pot and throw in some black pepper. I wonder if Hank realizes he doesn't have to work for an answer here. When he speaks, I remember that his shyness, his wanting to do and say the right thing, is what I first noticed, and liked, about him.

"Oh, you know. This and that," he says. "Listen, by the way, I wanted to ask you about something. I've been reading about near-death experiences? You know, when people die for a few minutes and then come back?"

"Like you almost did," I say. In the ensuing silence, I shake Tabasco sauce into the pot.

"Yeah. Well, not exactly. Anyway, I wanted to ask, do you think there's anything to it? All these people, the ones who've died or

into the middle of the pool's cold, dark silence. Then the small (
my back crunched on sand and I kicked free of the ball I'd made (
my body. Pushing off hard, I arrowed to the surface. Hank was aj
proaching the ledge I'd jumped from.

"Come on in, the water's *freezing*," I called.

Ignoring this, Hank gathered my clothes together.

"Hey! Don't wrinkle that blouse," I yelled. "I spent all afterno(
ironing it."

"Sorry."

"Ha-ank, I'm jo-king," I sang.

"Okay."

"Why don't you come in? I'll show you how to do the ba
stroke," I said, and demonstrated: flipping onto my back, I glic
to the opposite side on long, elegant strokes. By the time I'd wij
the water from my eyes, Hank was lighting a cigarette, his face f
ing paper-white in the lighter's flame.

"Hey, cowboy," I shouted across the water. "Get your boots
This offer expires at midnight."

Hank peered into the dimness of the forest but there was no
to see or hear us.

"Hank," I called, "please come swimming with me."

Hank slowly took off his jacket to my cheers and catcalls. Bu

"You can use this to dry off with," he said, dropping his jacke
the rocks. "Come on, Beth. Come on, now. You're drunk."

My arousal totally chilled, I inched back across the pool f
wise and climbed onto the ledge. Hank had turned away pri
just as if he'd never seen me naked. *And considering that we've al
made love in the dark*, I thought, *maybe he never really has*. I pi(
up his jacket and brushed it over my body, observing as I di
Hank's back, a dry expanse of white cotton with a single curl
of dark piping lazing between the shoulder blades: the shirt v
gift from me. I slipped on my underwear and jeans and slicke(
hair from my face.

"Okay, honey, I'm decent now," I said. "I don't know what (
over me."

whatever, they all say the same thing afterwards. That they were in some sort of tunnel or hallway, moving toward a light, and they meet people they've known who've died, *really* died."

For something to do with my hands, I chop some onion. "Maybe," I say, "it's the light at the end of the tunnel."

"I think Hank's being serious," Joellen says.

"No, really, Beth," Hank says. "It's true. These people all say there's nothing to be afraid of—that it's beautiful, really beautiful."

"Everything is *beau-ti-ful*," I sing, "in its own *waaay*."

Joellen is still looking at me. "What's the matter, Beth?"

"*Nothing*. But I don't see it. If you're dead, you're dead, that's all. I just can't believe people are really, honestly dying and then popping back to life. What are they, zombies? It doesn't make sense." I kill some jalapeños with a butcher knife, throw them, seeds and all, into the pot.

"But that's what I'm *saying*." Hank spreads his arms. "It's a mystery, a matter of faith. That's why," he says, turning to Joellen, "I'm asking you. You're a very religious person. What's your perspective on this?"

Joellen sips her wine. Her hair gleams, backlit by the light over the stove. "I suppose it could be a state of grace. Or a chemically created illusion or blind of some sort—somebody said this. Like a substance released by the brain that kills the fear of death? But my personal feeling is that the light these people describe is the light of God's eye. That when we die we go back into God's eye, just as we once came out of it."

"Whoa, yeah," Hank says.

"Or it's a trick of the devil's," Joellen says.

Julian appears in the doorway. His grin is huge. "Speak of the devil!" he shouts.

⁓

Halfway through dinner the telephone rings and Joellen picks up the kitchen extension. She stands at the counter for a moment, not saying anything, then turns to me with round eyes. "I think this must be for you."

I know who it is before I take the phone. Lauren talks to me for a long time, making no sense: a blizzard of words comes down the line. "Tell me where you are," I insist. More babble, then a druggy blare of music and rattle of pool cues.

"Where are you? Laurie, honey? Where are you?"

She doesn't know where she is, or she's not telling. But she confides to me that she has always wanted to carve a poem on her face with a razor blade.

"Where the hell are you?"

Lauren's voice chatters away from the receiver. A man's voice comes over the line roughly: "Yeah?"

"Yes," I say. "Where is she? What's happening?"

"Hell if I know. I was hoping you'd tell me, doll. She's *out* of it, is what's happening. You better come over."

He gives me the name of the place—a bar on Sixth—and I repeat it in the silent kitchen.

"I know that place," Hank says. He looks scared.

"So do I," Julian says softly.

The man on the telephone is still speaking. ". . . she have any money? 'Cause she's had two drinks already."

Lauren's voice rises in the background, keeping ragged time with the jukebox. Someone in the bar laughs. Some other son of a bitch claps.

I call the police, then my parents. My mother answers, breathless. "Oh, Beth, I was just trying to call you. Is she with you? Your father's out looking for her."

I tell her about the call from Lauren. Julian is intent, standing now by the kitchen door with my jacket in his hands. His lips are moving. I check Joellen: she's praying, too, her eyes are closed and she's holding Hank's hand; the fingers of her other hand are running blindly over his knuckles. And Hank—poor boy—looks at me helplessly.

"You should *see* this," my mother says. Her breathing is harsh, panicked. "She's poured water all over her room. I noticed a drip in the living room ceiling and when I came up she was pouring water into the window frames and along the baseboards. Into the frames! Her bed, the carpet, everything's soaked. It's all ruined. Everything's *ruined.*" She begins to cry. "She's been acting strange for days but what else is new? I heard the water running and running upstairs. I thought she was taking a *shower.* Everything's completely ruined."

"Mother, I have to go look for Laurie."

"I told your father to check her into Mercy, *for good,* this time. I can't take this anymore."

"Mother, don't—"

"Beth, the carpet *squishes* when you walk on it."

≈

Julian and I see the pulse of blue lights as we turn onto Sixth. "Lord God," he says quietly.

A few people have straggled out of the bar, drinks in hand, to watch as Lauren is escorted to the waiting car between two young policemen. When one of them puts his hand on her head, Lauren ducks as if burned, jackknifing into the back seat. Julian pays for her drinks while I give the policemen names, addresses, history.

I climb in beside Lauren, who rocks vigorously as the car pulls away, as if to urge it to greater speed, but by the time we roll through Mercy's gates her systems are shutting down; her hand, when I take it, is cool and limp. The hospital's bright, blank windows slide past. Somewhere along the line Lauren's parted company with her shades and her eyes, no longer shielded by smoked glass, close. We lead her—me on one side, a policeman on the other—up the steps and through the electric doors. Lauren slumps into a wheelchair. She doesn't speak to me or to anyone, not even to the tired doctor who asks her to open her eyes and look at him.

≈

It's after midnight and raining when Julian lets me out in front of the house. Exhausted but hungry, we'd stopped for coffee and dough-nuts after leaving my dad in the hospital parking lot, and now I'm clearheaded, light-footed, and stumbling all at the same time. I dash into the house by the kitchen door, take off my shoes, and negoti-ate the stairs in the dark.

My heart sinks when I hear Joellen's voice: she's waited up and now she'll want to talk or, worse, pray. She's in a state now, by the sound of it: a murmur, a ragged catch of breath, then a long, shapeless moan.

She's in the Last Supper Club. I follow the sound of her ecstasy down the hallway, my skin coming out in gooseflesh. And while I'm disinclined to disturb her, I follow an irresistible impulse and gently push the unlatched door open.

Joellen is kneeling in the middle of the room, facing the window. Her back is to me and her nakedness, in the dreamy, filtered moonlight, is a shock. She has her arms wrapped around herself and sways from side to side, moaning, a crazy woman embracing herself before God, and for a terrifying moment her head appears to double—to become two heads.

Then my eyes adjust to the dimness and I see that the arms wrapped around Joellen's back are not her own.

They're Hank's.

The other head belongs to Hank, too. His eyes are closed as he kisses her neck.

I back out of the room slick as a crayfish, and as I stand there listening to my heart pound, something Julian said earlier tickertapes across my mind. Paralyzed for the moment—literally unable to think or move—I fix all my attention on this.

We'd taken our coffee and doughnuts to the truck to avoid the shop's blaze of antiseptic light, and sat talking. Julian had a simple answer to the question of the back-from-death phenomenon.

"It's just a damn lie," he said, his words skimming steam from his coffee. "Read your Bible: does it say anywhere in it that you can slip your soul on and off like a T-shirt? Hell, no."

I began to protest but he waved it away.

"Look, I don't care what anybody says, it's not *my* idea of death. When *I* go, I intend to shoot out of my body like a rocket, sugar, and never look back."

Now, standing in the darkness of the hallway, I consider what to do. Shoot out of the house like a rocket? I could confront them if I had the guts. But I turn away from that, as I try to turn away from my sister's illness, away from Hank, away from being forever and ever alone. *Never look back,* Julian had said. But as the sounds of Hank's and Joellen's lovemaking become more pronounced, I realize that I have looked neither backward nor forward: rejecting the possibility of either heaven or hell, I am left without even a devil to instill in me the fear of a God I cannot make visible.

But I shake free and stomp to my room, taking no care of the noise I make.

In bed, suddenly limp, I burrow under the blankets. I imagine springing Lauren from Mercy: We take off for the Coast, me driving, Lauren talking. We slip into Mexico, find a village on the Baja where Lauren's held in awe by simple, adoring peasants. We live on beans and tortillas. The strange sisters slowly brown to the color of baked adobe, slip in and out of faulty Spanish over a deck of cards, pair of beers . . .

I wake up at first light, the lurid sunset of my expatriate dream fading, and hear footsteps in the hall. Joellen slips into the room, alights on the corner of my bed, tilting its geometry slightly—and for some reason this gesture of wobbling but unexpected intimacy slides a weight off my heart.

"You might knock first," I say.

"Sorry." Joellen droops, and her disheveled, golden hair folds like wings around her face. Her voice, when she speaks, is tiny. "How's Lauren?"

"I don't know. Crazy. Well-sedated, I'm sure. How's Hank?"

Little voice: "I sent him away."

"Ah."

Silence drains into the bedroom, filling it.

Joellen stirs. "I don't know how it happened," she murmurs. "We were going to pray for Lauren. He said he wanted to, so we went upstairs. And it occurred to me"—her voice rises and her eyes shine in the new light—"it came to me, as we were praying, that only love would save her. And I began to burn." Joellen looks into my eyes. "Do you know what I mean?" she says softly.

I try to remember a time when I have burned for love, but can't. In my mind I see only the tip of a candle's flame, the bright upright finger that says *no—not yet.*

≈

I still have my key and enter my parents' house quietly enough, but when I reach the top of the stairs Dad's waiting for me.

"Christ, Beth, what time is it?" His voice is thickened with a heavy rheum of sleep, and when I hug him I seem to feel the years of accumulating fatigue in my arms. "Early," I say. "I'll make some coffee."

But before I do, I visit Lauren's room. Mother's right: The carpet squishes. The room's become a damp, cool cell. Water from Lauren's spree, seeping into the plaster, has given rise to a dark wash of vaguely floral patterns that climb the ancient, lined wallpaper like a trellis. Lauren's garden appears to be growing before my eyes.

≈

I've decided to move—to go back home, at least for a while. Lauren's been home from the hospital for a month, everything's quiet. Dad's putting her room back in shape; until then, we sisters will share a room.

When I went to see her in Mercy, she was hanging out in the dayroom. She was calm and coherent but detached, accepting without a word my gift of a new pair of shades. I asked her—for once, I seemed to be doing most of the talking—if she remembered what she'd done to her room. She didn't say anything for a moment, just stared at me, her shades the chilly dark of night windows.

"I don't know if I'd call it a memory. I was pretty high. My feet were wet." She shook her head, looking annoyed. "What do *you* remember?"

"About what?"

"Anything," Lauren said, lighting a cigarette. "Do you remember, for instance, being born?"

"Of course not."

"I do," Lauren said. She took off her shades and polished the lenses on the sleeve of her T-shirt. In the dayroom's uncompromising light, she looked middle-aged and ill. But she smiled slyly. "Talk about a memory," she said.

"Fuck you," I said, and I smiled, too.

"Tell you what, Beth," she said. "I want to ask you something. Do you believe in God?"

"Yes." I imagined a distant, fabled relative I'd never met who loved me for no reason, whose love was not so much unrequited as unimaginable, almost comforting.

"Good. Pray for me," she said. Then shrugged, her smile struggling back. "Or don't."

I was brought up to believe that praying meant asking for something. When I was a child I prayed for a doll with shining hair and long, glossy limbs, for happiness, for what I thought of as "world peace," for the health of my family—and that they would not be taken from me. And when Lauren was taken away, I prayed on the way home from my first visit to the locked ward where Lauren sat laced and buckled into a straitjacket, spitting at our father as he approached her. By the time we arrived home, I had squeezed my heart so tightly that I imagined it had become a perfect stone, and I never prayed again.

All my things are packed in boxes. Lauren and Joellen and I are sitting in the kitchen having a last beer, waiting for Julian to come by with his truck. We're a somber trio. Joellen, although more quiet than usual, looks alternately pleased and distracted, and I wonder whether Hank is getting the guitar lessons he so deserves.

I need to get some things I'd stored in the basement, but when I go down there I discover only one lightbulb works: most of the stairway, and all the far end of the basement, is black. The watchful darkness conjures a memory of childhood monsters; foolish as I feel, I can't bring myself to go in there alone, so I trudge back up to the apartment. We find a flashlight that turns out to be as dead as its downstairs relations.

"I'll go," Lauren says. "I'm not afraid of the dark." She drops her shades onto the table and stubs out her cigarette. We walk single file down the stairs beneath the one working lightbulb and enter the cold room. I intend to go first as long as Lauren's coming with me, but when we reach the edge of the yellow skirt of light, Lauren comes up beside me and our shadows merge. She takes my hand.

"This is nothing," she says.

I hear footsteps on the stairs, then see Joellen slipping through the gloom. I can't read her expression as she moves toward us, but when she takes my other hand I see all at once a vision of the fireworks of my own death—far off or near, but always present—and my soul lifting off splendidly, piercing the darkness, a brilliant, inextinguishable rocket, a snap of sharp colors crinkled like tissue paper against the night sky.

"There isn't much to be afraid of," Joellen whispers.

We walk together into the chilly tank of darkness, the apostle, the lunatic, and the one whose fingers must see, whose eyes must touch, to believe. Over our heads, this house of prayer looms, vast and silent. I close my eyes and walk blind, letting them lead me. In a few moments Lauren flicks her lighter and I feel the feather of flame beating against my eyelids, but I don't open my eyes right away. Not just yet. I want to savor a long moment of darkness before I see my way again.

Physical Wisdom

In the spring of the year that we moved from Chicago to Loma Feliz, California, I began to be afraid to sleep indoors.

I was sixteen, living with my parents in the house my father had rented after walking away from a well-paying job with a Chicago psychiatric firm—his words—to take a civilian position at Camp Pendleton, counseling marines who'd had second thoughts about serving their country. I understood, as we packed the rental truck with the things we hadn't sold, that my father had taken a step down in the world. But this knowledge didn't jibe at all with his cheerfulness as he stood high in the back of the opened-up truck, looking both clumsy and powerful stripped to a T-shirt and cutoffs, flexing his white, heavy arms and slapping his hands together impatiently as I struggled toward him with yet another load.

August was nearly done. A layered, warm-and-chilly wind blew in from Lake Michigan, flipping what was left of my father's hair across the smooth crescent of his bald spot. I was to start school, in California, in a week.

They're modern parents. Talk, talk, talk. They'd asked me what I *felt* about moving—and what could I say? Wasn't it already decided? My father laid a map out on the kitchen table and reached way across America to the dot that was Loma Feliz, a town so small its name had been edged offshore where it drifted, an orphan in the blue Pacific. I scanned the intervening space—the vast, empty squares of the western states—while my father described our new home: a "vintage" ranch fifteen minutes' walk from the ocean. Avocado trees in the backyard. A large, bougainvillea-covered shed that my mother, at that time a painter of sensual reinterpretations of biblical themes—her Mary Magdalen was less than entirely penitent—planned to set up as a studio.

≈

"Robert, are you awake?" My father nodded absently, straining his attention westward, intent on getting us to a motel before night fell. Anchored between us, my mother squeezed my hand to let me know she was happy. I looked out at the dimming, surreal desert landscape and felt sure I would never see a tree again—a real tree. I remembered avocados from the supermarket in Chicago: the size, heft, and weight (I guessed) of hand grenades.

≈

My father drove north to Camp Pendleton every weekday morning at seven. Mom needed more time to get started. She routinely dumped the breakfast dishes into the sink and made a second pot of coffee, poured a cup for me, then sat quietly at the kitchen table, wrapped in the camouflage of an exotic, flowered robe, smoking the cigarettes my father couldn't abide and gathering herself for her day's work.

I walked to school through the village in the cold morning sunlight—not cold by Chicago standards, but damp. By afternoon, when I walked home, the sky would be bright, glaringly blue, and the day hot. On the hottest days, it was really only when you got close enough to the ocean to hear the breakers' echoing aftershocks that the air cooled.

Coming home one day I stumbled; I thought I'd caught my shoe in a crack in the sidewalk. But suddenly I seemed to be drunk, or what I thought drunk was: I lurched and nearly fell. Then I lost my balance and fell down. My books tumbled out of my arms, one of them opening neatly on the grass.

The earth was moving. I sat on the ground and felt the world trembling; beneath my hands I felt its hairy body shaking with tremendous mirth. A radio was playing in a nearby house and the music, a waltz, floated strangely on the air as the earth shook. I heard a woman calling a man's name. Telephone wires twitched as if teth-ered to invisible, restless dogs. The sky's inverted bowl of unshake-able blue burned over me. Birds raced in all directions.

Then it was over.

When I ran down our street a few minutes later, my mother was waiting for me in the front yard. She was dressed in her paint-crust-ed coveralls and still held a brush in her hand.

"Hey! Are you okay?" Her eyes were wide. She was happy, all right. She clapped her free hand dramatically to her heart and looked up and down the street. She would have liked to share her excitement with the natives, but we seemed to be the only people out of doors.

"*Carl*. Our first earthquake! Well—strong tremor? But that counts. We're really Californians now. Okay?" She put her hand on my head, stroking my hair. "Carl?"

"Yeah," I said. "It was neat."

But that was a lie. It hadn't felt neat at all. I couldn't catch my breath, and I kept sensing flashy, furtive movements at the edge of my vision and turning my head to catch them. I had slipped into a universe that wouldn't stop moving.

Panic had hit me in the stillness after the tremor. I had run the few remaining blocks home, and now I felt that I wanted to keep running: only swift movement would pacify the tremendous power that was pressing against my skin from inside. Running would con-ceal the shaking I felt certain was visible to my mother.

"Carl," she said, her voice low. "Honey. It's okay." Her hand slid lightly over the back of my head. She gingerly rubbed the place be-tween my shoulder blades where an evil current flashed sparks down my spine, plucking at the muscles of my arms and legs.

"I'm sorry," I said.

My mother spoke softly. "*No*." Keeping her hand on my back, she moved to my side and we stood together facing the house, listen-ing (I thought) to the noise of my breathing. When it quieted, she said, "Let's go in. I'll fix you something."

We had reached the front door when I remembered my books.

"Okay," she said. "Hm. Okay. You go and get them. Or—" a flourish of the brush—"I could come with you?"

"No, Mom, I'll go. I'll be right back. Thanks."

"All right, Carl." She smiled at me—and the earth began to shake again.

Seconds later it was over. I extricated myself from my mother's arms and together we walked back to where my books lay. I gathered them up and we walked home. I did not speak, but my mother, who loved California suddenly, all at once, and just like that, remarked brightly on the varieties of its flowers and trees—the flush of life surrounding us. But all I could see, in spite of her enthusiasm, was a deceptive veil of vegetation concealing an angry and treacherous earth.

I entered my bedroom that night with suspicion but everything was as I had left it in the morning. There were no signs of violence: the walls stood smoothly upright, the windows were intact. I had assigned reading, but once in bed I found I couldn't concentrate on the material.

My father had come in upset from work. A young marine in his care had jumped from a third-floor barracks window, breaking a leg and fracturing his skull. When the boy recovered, my father said with a tight and angry smile, he stood a good chance of being court-martialed for trying to kill himself. During dinner, my mother mentioned the tremor—which the news people were calling an earthquake—but my father only said distractedly, "Oh? We'll have to expect those, I suppose." I didn't say anything—didn't tell my father that I felt I had been pushed from a high place and was still falling—and we passed the rest of the evening in a gloomy silence.

When I switched off the bedroom light, my fear returned refreshed from where it had been working out. I began to sweat. As my eyes adjusted to the darkness, I made out the familiar outlines of the windows, the long, ghostly panels of the closet door shimmering into shape, the front edges of my desk brushed with a single stroke of light from the street. But it was all unfamiliar, too; it could've been any room. Like the motel rooms we stayed in on the trip west, its uniqueness had been stolen. Feeling on those nights an eerie kinship with a silent, migratory procession that had no beginning and no end, I had told myself, *It's just a motel room,* and then I had slept.

But I didn't sleep now. When I considered switching on the light for comfort, I felt ashamed and angry. The room seemed to sense this weakness and its hatefulness hardened into glee. I lay rigid, staring at the ceiling without blinking until its plastered creaminess deepened into a wavering illusion of troubled water. But when I rubbed my eyes and looked again, it was once again a solid surface, and more sharply focused. Just as I turned my head, something up there caught my eye.

I took the flashlight from the drawer of the night stand and followed its beam across the ceiling until it fixed on what I had spied: a long, meandering crack that cut right across the plaster.

Taking my pillow and blanket—and, after a moment's thought, the flashlight—I crawled under the bed. I set my mind on waking up at my father's first stirrings, and then I slept.

≈

My new friends Henry and Paul were talking about the quake in school the next morning. Henry, whose locker was next to mine, slammed it shut and leaned against the metal door.

"Hey, Carl, did you feel it yesterday?"

"I did."

"So?—what did you think?"

I shrugged and twirled the locker's dial.

"Man, that was *nothing,*" he said.

"It was less than nothing, dickweed," Paul said. "A *negative* quake." He looked at me. "You don't have quakes back east, do you?"

"Chicago is pretty stable," I said.

Henry drummed on his locker. "The big one! It's the big one! We're all gonna die!"

"Women and children first!" someone shouted, and everyone laughed. I twirled the dial.

"Yeah," Paul said. "Far out, man. When the big one comes, this place'll be history."

"So will *we*," Henry said. "Tidal waves, you name it. Look at this guy. Been here three months and can't get his locker open." He looked around. "Hey, *Carolyn*," he called, "by any chance do you know Carl's combination?"

Carolyn Wilson looked over from her open locker, smiled, and shook her head. She didn't have to speak, and we all knew it.

"This damn lock is broken," I said to Paul.

"You're pathetic, man," Henry said. "Hey, *Carolyn*, help this guy out." She was walking by. She was slowing down.

She actually stopped. We all froze.

"What seems to be the trouble, gentlemen?"

Cool and beautiful. Shoulder-length hair the colors of washed-out rock maple leaves in October. Freckles in a constellation across the nose. Smart, I had heard. *And you*, I thought, *you spent the night under the bed.*

"Beats me," Henry said. "Chicago here seems to be locked out of his locker. It's puzzling."

"Broken," I croaked.

"I see, said the blind man." She grinned at me.

The bell rang. Doors opened and the hallway was immediately, loudly jammed. She moved off, still smiling, and I jumped at this lingering contact.

"So what'll I do?" I called out.

"Suffer," she called back.

My father lowered his fork and looked at me across the table.

"Sleep out? What in the world for?"

I shrugged. "Why not? It's California, Dad. It's not like I'll get frostbite."

My mother didn't say anything. She ladled some more California-style vegetarian stew onto Dad's plate. Then she caught my eye:

we held our look for a moment—my gaze bland, hers appraising—before she turned to Dad.

"What can it hurt, Robert? Sounds healthy to me." She looked down. "This needs something. Cheese?"

"I love cheese," my father said. "I'd kill for cheese. Carl, check the fridge."

I fetched the cheese and grater and a bowl and brought them to the table, grated the cheese, and passed the bowl to my father. "So, can I?"

"What? Oh, sure." He heaped cheese onto his stew. "Better wrap up, though. Nights are surprisingly chilly out here . . . Oh, this definitely helps. Delicious."

"I think next time I'll use more pepper," my mother said.

"Carl, get the pepper," my father said.

My mother glanced up. "You're full of orders tonight."

"Can't help it," my father said. "Semper fi."

Mom sighed, got up, and brought coffee to the table. She poured cups for herself and my father.

"How about me, too, Mom?"

"None for you tonight, Carl." Again, that appraising look. "It might keep you awake."

I unrolled my sleeping bag and lay down on it, letting my gaze drift upward through the branches of the avocado trees and blowing clouds to the stars. I thought about Carolyn Wilson and felt foolish, happy, and relatively safe.

The back door opened and closed, and I heard the click of my mother's lighter. In a moment she came into view. She opened her hand and a stocking cap fell onto my stomach.

"Your father insists that you wear this."

"Okay." I put the cap on. I hadn't worn it since Chicago and already it seemed like an odd hand-me-down, a token from another life.

We'd spent our last day there visiting with my grandparents, and after we'd said good-bye my mother ran back and held her father and cried while I stood in the middle of the yard, waiting, and my father sat in the truck with the motor running.

"Great," I said. "Thanks."

"You're welcome." She took a drag from her cigarette. "Carl, what are you *wearing*?"

"My sweat suit."

"It's not enough. Really, you'll freeze. Come in and put something else on."

"Mom. I'm not even in the bag yet. When I get inside, I'll be fine."

My mother yanked her sweater tight around her shoulders. Her head was in the stars. "You *won't*. I won't have you catching pneumonia just because you insist on, I don't know, returning to a state of nature. I think it's going to rain."

"Oh, for Christ's sake, Mom."

After a moment she said, "I suppose I'll have to get used to being sworn at, too."

"Mom, I'm sorry. Look—I'm fine, really." I had no intention of moving.

"Forget it." She turned and started back toward the house. Then, as if to herself: "You're fine, I'm fine, we're all *fine*. Goodnight." She got halfway to the house before she stopped. She spoke in a voice almost too low to be heard but which carried, like the layered wind off Lake Michigan, mixed tones, warm and cool. "Call me if you need anything."

≈

I had already considered the possibility of rain and had a plan ready so that when, in the middle of my third night outdoors, I woke up with rain in my face, I quickly bundled up my bag and ran up the path to my mother's studio.

In the event of an earthquake, I reasoned, the shed would dance a little but would not collapse. Turning on the light, I surveyed the interior of the ten-by-twenty all-wood—therefore flexible—building. Nailed to one of its long walls and framed by windows on either side was my mother's new painting, of Saint Matthew composing his gospel.

According to legend, Matthew was illiterate, and wrote his gospel under the tutelage of an angel. Most of the classical pictures show him puzzling over a piece of paper while a studious and obliging angel stands nearby, guiding his hand toward enlightenment.

But my mother's saint has dropped his paper and pen and stares in astonishment at the decidedly female angel who's sitting on his lap. Their mint-perfect profiled heads all but touch at the nose and a yellow light shimmers from their hair, which appears, at first glance, to be in flames. You sense that only one or two moments have passed since the angel's appearance. But Matthew has regained composure enough to hook one arm securely around her waist and twist his fingers into the braided gold of her belt, anchoring her; and her right arm is flung around his neck, her fingers are already interwoven with his hair. At the exact center of the picture, she touches his lips with the fingers of her other hand, daring him, with her eyes, to speak the truth.

I spread my bag on the floor in the dark and crawled inside. Listening to the rain's impatient fingers on the roof, I fell asleep thinking about the possible kinship of women and angels, about my mother's saint catching fire, and, briefly, about how and when I would return to my own bed.

~

My mother was not at all pleased that I'd spent the night in the studio.

"You were breathing turpentine fumes all night," she said. "Don't you know how dangerous that is?"

"I didn't even notice."

This wasn't true: I'd woken up at six with a sharp pain jimmying my ribs.

"You should have noticed."

It was Saturday. We were all sitting at the kitchen table.

"Carl, I have to agree with your mother," my father said.

"You're in there all day," I said, ignoring him.

"I keep the windows open."

"So did I."

There was a silence. I lowered my eyes, but not before I caught the glance that passed between them. I drank my coffee, breathing shallowly so as not to awaken the turpentine cough that lay coiled at the end of each inhalation.

"Carl." My father leaned forward. "Marian and I have talked this over—now, don't misunderstand me. We respect your feelings about the earthquake and we know you're apprehensive. Maybe—"

"Oh, you've talked it over. That's great," I said. To avoid their anxious eyes I looked at the window, running with California rain.

"Carl—"

"Just call me Chicken Little."

"Carl? Hon?" my mother said.

"Old Yeller," I said.

"Absolutely not," my father said. "You're being hard on yourself for no reason. What you're going through is by no means uncommon."

"I'm not one of your psycho patients, Dad."

"*Carl.*" My mother's incantation was a whisper.

"No, clearly not." My father stood up. "You're my son. Do what you have to do."

I stood up, too, but I didn't know where either of us was going. My mother remained seated. Her red flowery wrap with its deep, extravagantly cuffed sleeves gave her the appearance of a mandarin. She seemed about to pass sentence.

"The studio is off limits," she said.

"Okay."

"It's mine," she added. "Not yours, not ours. Mine."

"Fine."

"Just so you understand," she said, and rose from her chair. She began to pile the breakfast dishes deliberately and loudly into the sink, and my father and I went our separate ways.

≈

As I exited Bauman's Outfitters that afternoon, I swerved to avoid running into Carolyn Wilson, who was entering.

"We meet again," she said. "Going camping?"

"Hi. Yes. Well, sort of."

She grinned and gestured widely with her dripping umbrella. "You've got the perfect day for it."

I shifted the bulky package containing my new tent to my other arm. An escaping pair of metal-tipped tent poles made a swipe at Carolyn and missed, then clattered onto the sidewalk. I bent to retrieve them, and several more fell out. Then they all fell out.

"Whoops," she said.

I gathered the poles together and stood up, dizzy with embarrassment, crushing the wet and disintegrating bag to my chest.

"Not really camping," I said. "Just—"

Carolyn was waiting, looking at me out of hazel eyes. Her eyebrows were brushed, like her hair, with red. Her smile was going to go, any minute now. She would vanish.

"My name is Carl," I said.

"*I* know. Carolyn," she said, putting out her hand and laughing. We shook hands.

"Would you like to go out sometime?"

"Sure. When?"

"I don't know." I really didn't know, but I had to keep talking. "I don't know," I said again, brilliantly. "But I'll call you."

"Great! I'm in the book."

I walked home slowly. The rain fell steadily, mildly, and I put my face into the sky and let it run into my eyes. I thought about nothing at all except how she had held her umbrella over both our heads the whole time we were talking.

≈

I had used my tent only twice when my parents told me I had to begin sleeping indoors again. My father offered to pay for the tent, which I had bought out of my savings, and I refused the money.

"Carl," my mother said, "listen to me. Once you sleep indoors one night, just one night, you'll see, I'm certain, that nothing's going to happen. Nothing."

"No," I said. "This house is going to fall down and I'm not going to be inside it when it does."

My father whipped off his glasses—a spectacular effect, one that I had seen before, though not often. He stared at me with myopic intensity.

"Good Christ," he said. "Aren't there enough real problems in the world without adding to them? Your sleeping outdoors simply isn't tenable anymore. Now make up your mind to it and let's have an end to this."

"Oh, it's real," I said.

"It *isn't* real," my mother said. "You've been scared and we want to help you. But you've got to meet us halfway."

"I'll sleep in the car."

"You will N O T sleep in the car," my father thundered. "You will sleep in the goddamned house beginning T O N I G H T."

That night I slept in the closet. I positioned myself so that my head and shoulders were within the shelter of the door frame. In order to accomplish this I kept the door open and slept on my side, contracting my body into a fetal position in the cramped space. I woke up feeling bruised and sore to find my mother standing over me.

"Oh, Carl, *Carl*," she said. "Breakfast is ready."

The following night I turned down my bed to discover that my mother had bought me new sheets: crisp, fresh-smelling, blue-striped cotton. Matching pillowcases.

I sat gingerly, reluctant to disturb the hotel-perfect fit. Doing so, I felt, would be an admission of some sort, a physical declaration of my intention to spend the night there. But it would force me, too, to face another fact: that I was no longer so afraid. I was now merely—and for some reason, shamefully—worried.

I rolled into bed fully dressed. Switching off the light, I closed my eyes for several minutes. When I opened them again my room's familiar features stood out in dim but ordinary relief. There, the window. There, the dresser. Up there, the crack.

A cool wind fluttered the curtains and I pulled the bedspread over me. My mind, strangely peaceful, ticked off my concerns in stately slow-motion as I turned over my worries:

I would never see my grandparents in Chicago again.

Carolyn, who seemed to like me, would suddenly cease to care.

My father would become chronically dissatisfied with his work and move us again and again.

I would be buried in an earthquake and die anonymously, needlessly, along with thousands of others who had gone on believing that everything was all right.

My mother, whom I loved, would also die.

I became aware of the silence in my room and of the noises darkly hidden within the silence: the *shush* of blood in my ears, the rhythmic thump of my heart when I placed my hands, one over the other, on my chest. Exhaustion and worry fell like twin pennies on my eyelids.

I dreamed that I was walking on a strange continent whose obelisk-shaped buildings poked their tiny upper stories through the clouds. I knew the buildings were empty because of the numbers of people walking over the grass in the oppressive, sunless heat. Everyone seemed to be talking at once and I couldn't make out individual words. But a needle of news threaded the heavy air, giving shape to a stifling rumor: I understood that an impending earthquake had sent everyone outdoors, and it further became clear that everyone's wish now was to escape the open areas that would fill with rubble when the skyscrapers collapsed. With a rising sense of confusion and panic, I fled into another dream:

I was on a road in a village at twilight. Bougainvillea vines climbed the walls of the adjacent houses; bunches of their blood-red, voluptuous leaves nearly overshadowed the road. At the end of the road stood a house with a single high, brightly lit window, and at the center of the window a woman stood framed. I ran toward the house with relief, shouting and waving, certain that the woman was my mother. But when I reached the house, I saw that the figure in the window was an angel—my mother's angel from the Saint Matthew painting—and that her eyes were brilliantly blue, and blind. She raised her hand in greeting or negation, then slowly drew the hand across her face.

⁓

I woke up before dawn and made my bed while light materialized in the room. My father looked in.

"You're up," he said with surprise. I finished dressing and followed him out to the kitchen.

"Coffee's ready. Marian's sleeping in." He sat down heavily, as if tired out by the effort of making these announcements.

"What's wrong?" I said.

Something wasn't right. He wasn't ready for work. He sat very still, his hands lying on the table like a pair of gardener's gloves.

"Did you sleep well," he said.

"Fine." I waited. "I'm going to sleep in my bed from now on. And I'm sorry for what I said, Dad, about your patients being psychos. I was out of line with that shit."

He nodded so slowly that I couldn't tell if he'd heard what I said. He seemed to be entranced. Then his hands came back to life and he waved one of them as if to clear the air.

"That's good," he said. "I know it was hard for you, Carl."

Heaving himself up, he went to the counter and poured a cup of coffee for me, then set it down on the counter and simply stared out the window.

"So, what's going on?" I said—and was suddenly afraid. "Dad, you didn't quit?"

"What?" He looked at me blankly. "Quit what? *Oh.* Quit my *job.*"

He began to laugh, one big explosion setting off the next, until he was leaning over the sink, shaking, his arms wrapped around his middle. Then, stopping as suddenly as he had begun, he ran the tap and washed his face. He lifted a fresh dishtowel from the drawer and wiped his face dry. His voice, when he spoke, was hoarse.

"That boy, the marine I told you about? The one who jumped from a window? He's dead. He killed himself in the hospital last night. Got into the dispensary and drank something—took something."

He folded the dishtowel into thirds as he spoke, smoothing it with the flat of his hand. "He had a second opportunity, and took it."

"God, Dad. I'm sorry."

He nodded. "So am I. Sorrier than I can say. I've been trying to figure out what I could have done." He brought his hands together, leaving a space between them that a face might have filled, or slipped through. "To prevent this. Eighteen," he said. "Good *Christ*." He dropped his hands and turned from the counter. "Your mother will probably sleep for a while. We were up so late. I have to leave in a minute." He rubbed his cheeks. "I'm unshaven, Carl. I forgot to shave."

I went to my father and put my arms around him, and his heavy arms fell over my shoulders like a landslide.

≈

After Dad drove off, I walked out through the early morning coolness of the backyard, let myself into my mother's studio, and stepped up to her painting. At first I could see nothing different. Then I observed the changes she had made since the last time I looked.

Although the angel still sat on his lap, Saint Matthew was now weeping. He continued to look astonished in spite of his troubled tears. And his angel, the original dare still alive in her expression, no longer touched his lips but instead reached a little higher with her outstretched finger—drawing out his tears in an effort, perhaps, to teach him a more fundamental language than he had bargained for.

≈

It was still too early to go to school, so I wandered down to the ocean. Walking out onto the broad beach I pulled my jacket tighter around my shoulders, feeling the wind beat down on me in short, hard gusts.

There was no one else in sight. Only an occasional gull-screech

cut through the steady roaring of the waves. The packed sand barely moved under the pounding of the surf, but as I walked farther
out it loosened, melting as the retreating water slurred and sucked
around my shoes.

The world was in constant, sometimes secret motion: I was moving—I hoped—toward Carolyn. My father was behind the wheel,
freshly shaven, heading north. My mother, still asleep, traveled toward morning in a dream.

I stood in the surf until my shoes nearly disappeared, the heels
digging in first, the toes tipping skyward. This was how I wanted to
go: a little at a time in a slow rush, not all at once, not missing anything. Stumbling backward, I regained my balance and ran back up
the beach with the wind beating around my head like giant wings.

Mountains of the Moon

About three-quarters of the way up the mountain, Mike began to fall behind. This was inevitable. Not only was he unused to hiking, or to any strenuous exercise, but he was outdistanced by the strength of his wife's desire. She had more than enough of that; she'd reach the top first. And Frank was right behind her. His van was parked where the dirt road ended, a thousand feet below them. With half a mile to go, Mike stopped, leaned his weight against a tree, and watched their backpacks disappear into the leaves along the trail above him.

Mike and Katy met at a race seven years earlier—a fundraiser at the school where Katy taught fifth grade. She was warming up, stretching her tanned athlete's legs, when Mike walked up to her and struck up a conversation. Katy asked him if he ran. "Only if someone's chasing me," he replied.

When the race was over, Mike caught up with Katy in the parking lot. He had seen her win—he'd seen her flash of determination at the finish—and now he asked her out. She thought for a moment. A strand of hair which had escaped her ponytail lay smoothed with sweat along the length of her nose. She lifted the strand, examined it, cross-eyed, then plastered it across her forehead and said, "Yeah, okay."

"Okay, then," Mike said. "Terrific. I'll call you."

They went out twice that week. Then Katy came along when Mike took his nephew trick-or-treating. Mike and Katy stood holding hands in the damp leaves at the curb as the boy, draped sadly in a sheet, carried his bag from one porch to the next. Jack-o-lanterns, yellow-eyed, grinned at them in the dark.

On their fifth date, Katy asked him to spend the night. He never really went home. Three months later, Katy became pregnant, and six months before their daughter, Alison, was born, they were married.

≈

"It's not a big mountain," Frank had assured him over lunch the day before. "Not *too* big, but a good hour's climb. Steep, too."

"How steep is steep?"

"It's a *mountain*. It gets vertical. You'll love it."

Mike stepped into the clearing at the top of the mountain and reflected that, so far, he had not loved any of it. His swollen feet felt steamed, as if the sweat that had poured out of him on the climb had drained into his shoes. But his upper body felt light; he seemed to have shed excess weight as well as water. He stripped off his backpack, settling it on its lopsided bulge of a six-pack, sandwiches, and chips, and lit a cigarette.

Mike and Katy had known Frank once upon a time—he'd come into their lives in a crisis, when they'd needed him, or someone like him—and now here he was again. Frank had been a priest, and then, within a year, he'd quit the priesthood and turned up in Mike's office, looking for work. *What can you do?* Mike had asked. He was at a loss as to what to do with a guy who had spent the greater part of his life praying. A guy who had sat in his living room and watched him cry. *I can learn*, Frank had replied. And he had.

Then Katy had gotten interested in climbing, and it turned out that Frank, the Northeast's answer to Saint Francis, had been tramping around the woods for years, and their friendship opened up, and Mike was left behind the door that had opened. All the outdoorsy types Katy met were gregarious and sturdy. Katy's circle of friends widened. Mike had no friends except for Katy.

"I need to mix with other people, now," she told Mike one night after they'd lain awake very late, unable to make love or to sleep. "I need that like you wouldn't believe."

"So, mix," Mike said.

Katy was leaning on her elbow. Her silhouette loomed darkly, an undulating landscape, in the periphery of Mike's vision.

"It's not just that, Mike. If I don't get out of here soon, I'll be lost, too."

≈

This summer she'd climbed all the mountains up to Maine and back and twice gone out west with Frank and some others in search of tougher climbs. Both times it was a group affair.

At last, reluctantly, Mike bought a pair of hiking shoes.

≈

The top of the mountain was rock: long, submerged ellipses of white and purple lichen-encrusted granite that reminded Mike of the whale he'd once seen from the deck of a boat off the coast of Mexico. He'd watched in awe as the whale's gleaming, corrugated skin slid out from under the water. He felt a slight giddiness now as he walked along the raised backbones of the rocks. The tingling in his legs seemed to anticipate a senseless shift—the warning of an imminent sounding—that would throw him into the depths of trees he now stood above.

Mike spied Frank standing atop the mountain's highest outcropping of stone, nearly a quarter of a mile away. Frank stood with his arm outstretched, finger pointing; his legs were braced against the wind in the stance of an explorer. "Oh, holy one," Mike said to no one. Looking down and back, Frank crouched, then straightened, pulling Katy up to his level. They swayed, grabbing each other, and their laughter was blown, after a moment's delay, to Mike's ears. But the spark that lifted their voices into the air signaled their isolation, too, and after a moment they drew apart. When they spotted Mike, he already had his hand raised in greeting, and when Katy waved to him he imagined himself as she might have seen him: small and distant, with the wind slowly wearing down the mountaintop between them.

≈

"This is glorious," Katy said. She pulled off her windbreaker and sat, cross-legged, and emptied her backpack of her share of the lunch items. The sun's warmth slipped like minnows through the currents of the cool September breeze. Frank lay in the shade, his cap pulled down over his face. His sturdy legs stretched out into the sunlight that stopped where Mike sat uncomfortably against a tree, smoking. He had risen much too late that morning, putting them hours behind schedule, but neither Katy nor Frank had complained. No one had had much to say on the drive, either, and now the silence they had brought up the mountain unfolded itself again until it took up all space. Mike opened his backpack. "Who wants a beer?"

"Sure," Katy said.

Frank didn't move for a moment. Mike felt his waiting. They all felt themselves waiting.

"Whoa," Frank said then, and propped himself up on an elbow. "It'll probably put me to sleep, but thanks, yes indeed, I'll take one." He reached for a can of beer.

"I thought you were already asleep." Mike helped himself.

Katy held up sandwiches. "Frank, which? Tuna? Have something to eat."

"Yes, ma'am." Frank took off his cap and pushed damp, curly hair back over his narrow skull. "Gimme tuna. God, this is amazing, isn't it?" he said. "Let me ask you something. *Why* do you suppose we're the only people up here? Why is that?"

Mike drank half his beer and said nothing.

"Why do *you* think?" Katy asked.

"I don't know, I haven't any idea. But look here"—he extended his arms to present their surroundings, as if offering them bruised rocks, trees, and blue afternoon sky tinting sharply, in the west, to a seething spot of weather. "Here we are, no one around. Look at that sky. Magnificent! Of all the places anyone could wish to be, and on a day like this." Frank gathered his sandwich together with both hands and bit into it. "Oh, Katy, this is good."

"No trouble, padre."

"So I guess I don't know what people *do* on a day like this one," he continued, after taking another bite and glancing at each of the others. "Fight the crab grass? Watch a game on TV? Go to the mall?"

"Perhaps a stimulating combination of all three," Mike said.

"Oh—you," Katy said. She slapped his leg, which required that she lean across the sun-filled center of their picnic space. "You know what he means."

Frank spluttered, "*I* don't know what I mean!—I don't really know. It's hard for me to see what people want anymore, or why they want . . . whatever they want. People seem unaccountable to me."

"Unaccountable, how?" Mike asked.

Katy said, "I think Frank just means—"

"Yes, I was asking Frank what he meant."

"—that people are individuals, Mike. Okay? Unreadable." She took her eyes off her husband and looked at Frank. "Is that right?"

"Something like that," Frank said.

Mike lit a cigarette, relishing the disapproval in the set of their expressions. "Maybe what you mean, father, is that you wish people were more like you."

Katy whistled. "Oh *ho*," she said.

"No, it's true enough. That's fair," Frank said. "But let me ask you something, speaking of people like you and me and us: Would you have come along today if Katy and I hadn't insisted?" Frank had set his beer can in the dust and was pressing it into concentric patterns.

"Nope."

"What would you have done, instead, then?"

"Gone to the mall," Mike said.

"I think I'll go for a walk," Katy said.

"You mean 'a hike,' don't you?"

"Yes, Mike," she said without getting up to go.

Frank said, "Well, I'm certainly not complaining. Maybe I haven't been around people enough—been out in the world long enough—but if people don't want to come up here, it's fine with me. All the better, in fact. It's just for us, this way. Though I'd still like to share it, this gift of God."

"Amen," Katy said.

"I guess that depends on whether or not you believe in God," Mike said. He couldn't stop.

"*What?*" Katy said. "What does that mean? I mean—" She shook her head. "Never mind."

Frank said, "Everyone's free to believe whatever they want to."

"I know *that*," she said.

Mike looked at Katy. She hadn't said a word when she woke him that morning, just pushed on his shoulder until he opened his eyes. "What, then?" he asked. "What were you thinking? We're both interested. Aren't we, Frank?"

"Wait a minute. Let's just . . . wait a minute," Frank said.

Katy sighed. "I really am going for a walk."

"Okay."

"You know," she said. "I was just thinking that you said—I *thought* you said, once—that you believed in God. That's all. Didn't you? So I'm surprised because—this is ridiculous." She put her hands flat on the ground, preparatory to rising in a single unwinding upward motion. "Maybe I'm wrong, Mike. I just don't know."

"I don't know what could have made me say such a thing," he said. "I must have been out of my mind."

"You were, as a matter of fact."

He watched her as she rose and turned and walked off. He was sweating again, as if he'd been climbing the side of something impossibly steep.

"We don't have to turn this into a big thing," Frank said. "Mike? We really don't."

"I *like* malls," Mike said loudly. When Katy didn't turn around, he went on: "I *like* them because there are no goddamned *deerflies* in them."

"Michael," Frank said.

"Just shut up, *father*. You don't know shit."

"Man, I know I don't."

"Then just don't tell me, okay? Don't sit there telling me what a big thing it is or isn't, or anything. I like it there. I go there. I like it because there are lots of people—you getting this? People just keep walking around. There's no weather in there, no trees except for those ugly, skinny potted things."

"You're hurting Katy."

"Oh, that's great. I'm hurting Katy. That's really good," Mike said. "I'm warning you, Frank."

"It's the truth."

Mike felt himself fill, suddenly. He was a cold, bright container of hate and he would pour himself over Frank.

"The *truth*? You're going to tell me about the truth? You want to tell me what hurts? Try cutting off your hand and tell me if it hurts. I'll tell you what hurts, if you want to know and you think you can take it. You can have it. I'll give it to you." Mike was whispering. "You're nobody's father."

Frank was crying. "I love her, too," he said.

Katy was walking back to where they sat. But when she was within ten feet of them, she stopped and looked up. Her eyes opened wide. "Oh, my *God*."

The men scrambled up and went to her. Together they turned and looked up beyond the tree line at what she had seen: a full, ripe, lush yellow moon lifting free of the mountains.

～

Alison had been a year and a half old when Mike took her out to look at the moon.

She was playing in her room. Mike rushed in, picked her up and hurried back down the stairs, asking her, "Do you want to see the moon? Do you? If you do, say, 'Yes, Daddy.'"

Alison looked at him with incomprehension and approval. She had a wad of his shirt collar in her fist. "Yes," she said, nodding. Then, finding a rhythm, "YesYesYes."

Mike laughed and pushed the screen door open. "You have no idea what I'm talking about, right?"

"Yes, yes," the girl chanted.

The night was cooled by a breeze. The stars looked famished on the chilled black ice of the sky. Mike turned and pointed to the full, creamy moon. "There," he said. "See it? The moon. Isn't it beautiful? The moon, sweetheart, sweet baby. It's the moon."

Puzzled by his excitement, Alison looked up, first at his upraised hand, then beyond it. The moon!

Alison stared. Her tiny lips parted. After a moment, she closed her mouth and drew back, bowing, putting her arms around Mike's neck. Her body trembled in his arms. She began to cry. "Mommy," she cried. "I want Mommy."

〰

Mike left Katy and Frank and loped heavily over the rocks. When he stopped to breathe, he found he had reached the highest point of the mountain. Looking down on the sweep of treetops, he recalled a piece of trivia from third grade: that in the country's early days, before the Eastern forests had been cleared, a squirrel could travel from the woods of New England to the Mississippi River—tree to tree—without ever once touching the ground. He remembered the sense of awe he'd felt at this illustration of the young forest's vast, nearly limitless abundance, its impossible density—its ability to literally support an army of animals that need never, in its ceaseless search for food, risk the danger and darkness of solid earth. But now, as he stood above the trees, his eyes blind to what their billions of shadows concealed, he felt a surge of panic, which turned at once to a longing for Alison so intense he went to his knees. He lay against the backbone of rock. He could hear Frank's voice, then Katy's, answering. He felt sleep turning toward him as it often did, unexpectedly, in a warm, seductive rush. He had thought, a year ago, that he would have to endure sleeplessness, but he hadn't: he had slept, as he would sleep now. Sleep had been the ally that betrayed him to his enemy, the dream, and his enemy was always waiting. He closed his eyes.

〰

The yard stretched all the way to the trees. Alison ran with her ball down the long, green corridor, her braided hair flying. Mike marked her progress by the way her footprints in the grass flared with phosphorescence, a ghostly shimmer from the southern ocean where whales rolled their careless, giant bodies unseen beneath the stars. There were people in the trees. Mike moved uneasily beneath the canopy of their murmuring voices and Alison ran on, flinging her ball, throwing it higher and higher until finally it soared out of sight. The sky went dark. Voices rose high up on either side of the yard as the tree people shouted to one another, leaning out, their weight fluttering the lesser darkness in the branches as if a wind were passing through the trees. Look at that! *they shouted.* The moon! *Alison's ball, beautifully round and shining, floated down through the trees as if drawn by a string. Mike looked for her, but she was gone; her luminous prints, which faded as the ball waxed brighter and nearer, seemed to run in all directions, their color draining into the earth. Mike began to call to her but his words unraveled, drifting casually up into the darkness, catching like cotton in the branches of the trees.* The moon, *he heard himself say.* The moon!

≈

Mike and Katy continued to look for Alison in vain all that night, and all the next day and night. Search parties were organized; flashlights flickered deep into the woods near whose borders she had last been seen. Some of the searchers returned at daybreak, clutching their walkie-talkies, stumbling with fatigue and failure, but others, Mike among them, went on looking, along roads and across the fields and finally, without hope or sense, on into the old, high farming country of the previous century with its wild orchards and grassy, shoulder-deep cellar holes.

It seemed to Mike, exhausted and stricken but not yet grieving, that a vast exodus was taking place—that from where they had come, they could never return; that one day the searchers would walk out from under the cover of the enclosing forest to find themselves in the weak, dirty daylight on the banks of the placid Mississippi—the promised agony of safe passage concluded—and that since Alison had led them there, she would at last be found.

≈

When Mike opened his eyes, he saw Katy kneeling on the rock beside him. Frank was standing nearby, his face nearly eclipsed by the shadow his cap's bill cast in the fading light. The moon had risen higher; its yellow had burned away, exposing the true, white scraped-raw face.

"We'd better get started down," Katy said. She wiped Mike's face with her bandana, pushing her thumbs gently into the corners of his eyes. Then she tied the cloth around her neck and zipped her jacket to enclose it. "Feel that chill," she said. "Are you cold?"

"Yes," he said. "I feel it, now."

Katy looked up at the moon, but her hands went back to Mike; her fingers moved lightly over his chest, probing for evidence of where, exactly, his heart was buried. "It's like the sun, it's so bright," she said softly. "But not the sun. Not hot like the sun. Some mountains up there, I'll bet."

Frank hoisted his backpack onto his shoulders. "Let's go, buddy," he called. "We don't want to spend the night up here." He dropped toward the shadowy opening in the trees that would take them down to the van.

Mike watched as Katy closed and buckled her backpack and adjusted its straps before slinging it around and onto her back, then pulling the waist straps together and cinching them in a loose but secure bond. She moved her shoulders to settle her burden. When she had finished, she stood very still in the fading light.

"I'm ready to go, now," she said.

Invisible Waves

When Grandpa Ford says he'll die before he sees the Grand Canyon, he means it two ways: he doesn't want to look at a monument to erosion (except in the mirror, he says), and he figures he won't be around long enough, anyway, to be subjected to such a long trip. He lisps to Ginger's mother, "In a *car*? Do you hate me? Why not go all the way and rent an ambulance?" His mouth twitches, the slippery conch-shell pink of his gums gleams. Grandpa Ford has no teeth. When he's mad, like now, his lips tend to move in undisciplined gusts of anger.

A year ago he still had the full set, stained ivory-yellow from smoking. He still smokes, up in his room, in secret, he thinks. Ginger remembers sitting up on his bony thighs when she was little, breathing in that old man smell and reaching up to tap his teeth with her fingernails while he grinned and growled. "Careful, little girl," he'd say. "I'll bite 'em right off. I'm a lion. I could eat up everybody in this house."

But Ginger's mom isn't likely to be eaten up, not by him. Not by anybody. She doesn't say a word more, just hands him a paper napkin before Ginger can signal to him that there's a clot of oatmeal on his chin, and he scours his mouth with the napkin and stuffs it into the pocket of his bathrobe. Since the barium treatments, he's lost most of the feeling around his mouth and nose. He got well, but the procedure fried the nerve endings.

Grandpa Ford moved in with the family two years ago, the week Ginger turned eleven. He brought only a suitcase; he'd sold everything else. Ginger's dad said he had drawings dating from Renaissance Amsterdam in the trunk of his car, which in rage at his illness he forgot about, and they went with the car. A fortune, Ginger's dad said.

When she does his laundry, she collects his balled-up napkins, feeling ashamed. She counts them, and then she straightens up. Sometimes the napkins are bloody, but whether it's from his naked gums, or some deeper place, she doesn't know.

He claims he can't get to sleep anymore without music, and Ginger knows just what to do.

After school, she goes right up to Grandpa Ford's room. He's sitting in an easy chair by the window in his robe and pajamas, one leg cocked up over the chair's arm, drinking Scotch out of a teacup. "Did you bring it?" he asks. She hands over her transistor radio and earphone and he takes this permanent loan in cupped hands as if it were as light as the music that percolated through its circuits.

He was on the radio once, in California, a long time ago. "When I had a life," he lisps. His show was called "Ford Takes Five," and in her mind Ginger smoothes out his voice to what she imagines it must have sounded like then, talking that smooth late-afternoon talk and giving the weather report (sunny, warm) between spins of jazz.

Ginger lives for radio—can't get enough. But the only bands she wants to hear are rock and roll bands, the Beatles and the Stones, and when her parents go out she turns up the volume on the big Motorola and sits in front of the speakers with her eyes shut, imagining she's in the third row at the Royal Albert Hall, screaming her head off.

She's read about the hysteria and seen it on TV. Not just the screaming and fainting but worse: puddles of urine on the seats in the concert halls. Knickers—that spiky, utterly wrong foreign word—thrown onto stages. Girls going mad.

That night at dinner Ginger negotiates for an overnight with her best friend, Helen. Helen's mom is away, which means Helen's dad will have the girls fix his dinner. Then he'll watch the ball game on television until he falls asleep. "He's always tired," Helen says. "He'll last about an hour."

Then they're going out. But Ginger doesn't mention this to her mother.

Grandpa Ford cuts his meat into slivers and mashes his vegetable and potato into a chunky paste. He looks depressed; but why pretend to enjoy something you can't even taste? Ginger thinks he looks older, more spare than he did this morning, as if small hands had gleaned the bare field of his skin all day. Also, he's a little drunk. The radio she gave him is in his pocket and the acorn-shaped earphone is in his ear. Every now and then he drags his voice across a phrase of what he's listening to.

"I don't see why you can't go," her mother says. "Dad?" She means Ginger's father. *Her* father is in Florida, brown as a football, thriving.

Ginger's dad nods, cutting into his chop, and Ginger holds her breath: it isn't settled until they ask some questions. But just then Grandpa Ford raises his fork as if he's about to make an announcement—and begins to sing. It's pretty bad. The mother just looks at her plate and keeps chewing, but the father puts down his knife and fork. "Please," he says. "Dad, give it a rest, huh? Let's have a meal where nothing happens, okay? Can we do that?"

But something does happen, something wicked: Grandpa Ford contracts into himself, drops his fork, and coughs a wad of food about the size of a golf ball toward his water glass. Some blood splatters the tablecloth. Ginger's dad gets to his feet, quick, and takes his father by the shoulders, puts his mouth close to his ear: "Dad. Are you all right? Can you breathe?"

"My God," Ginger's mother says, and Ginger says, "Mine, too," and looks at her mother in a way that she hopes hurts.

Grandpa Ford sits with his eyes closed. He looks too tired to tremble, but all the pieces of him move as if an outside element were trying to rustle him together or shake him apart. There are fine red veins on his eyelids that are like roads on a map held at arm's length. He slowly moves his hand to cover his son's hand and Ginger's dad holds Grandpa Ford's head and kisses him. It's still just spring, but the days are already hot. The narcissus have all wilted along the fence out back where the yard ends and the woods begin. Grandpa Ford's earphone loosens and falls like a petal into his lap: an earful of saxophone squeaks. Then the world's smallest rhythm section begins to play.

Ginger parks her bike next to Helen's and goes in through the kitchen door.

"Hey."

"Hey also."

Helen's sitting at the table with a textbook in front of her. She smiles, then makes a face that says, "Can you believe this?"

Doing homework on a Friday night is Helen's cross to bear, as she puts it—her parents believe in business before pleasure. Or maybe they just believe in business. The radio on the counter plays Little Eva, and canned spaghetti sauce simmers on the stove. Ginger hears the murmur of a TV announcer's voice leaking in from the living room: *And here's the pitch . . .*

"I think he's got it again," she says.

Helen puts her finger on her place and looks up. "Who? What?" she asks.

They've been over all this, but Helen doesn't always listen. If you have cancer, and the drugs don't get it all, it can come spreading back, unseen: *metastasizing,* which sounds to Ginger like black feathers fanning out inside you, killing everything they touch, a silent rushing incoming tide. Ginger imagines Grandpa standing at the railing at the Grand Canyon, his skinny body turning darkly to shreds, the shreds becoming blackbirds and flying off over the abyss, their cries coming back more and more faintly until they disappear.

She'd left the house without any fuss. Her parents had put Grandpa Ford to bed and were in their bedrooom, talking, using the words Ginger'd heard them use before: *permanent, hospital, impossible, crazy, dying.* She stopped at the door to say goodnight. Her dad was lying back against the pillows, one arm up over his eyes. "Goodnight, Ginny, be good now." Her mother didn't say anything, just sat and smoked, her eyes on the window and a better picture than she was seeing here.

Helen goes over to where Ginger is standing. "What are they going to do with him?" she says.

"They're talking about a hospital or a home."

"God, I'm so *sorry,*" Helen says. But neither of them can imagine such places.

The girls set out plates and silver and put the spaghetti into water. They don't talk about Grandpa anymore—what's to say? Once upon a time, there was an old man who got so godawful sick he had to be put into a radioactive pressure cooker, kind of a glass coffin, children, and presto!—when he was done, his teeth floated to the top like kernels of boiled corn.

Ginger sits at the table and picks at the little scabs of fingernail polish that obscure the creamy half-moons rising from the root-end of the nail. She listens as Helen hums to the music on the radio and wishes she could *be* Helen. Inhabiting Helen's body, she thinks, would free her from the snake of sadness that twists through her like dark, slow water. Helen is safety.

Helen and Ginger kissed one night. They were having an overnight, like tonight, and they were goofing, practice-kissing their pillows, when Ginger had the idea that they should kiss for real. They put their lips together and pressed. Ginger had her eyes closed, of course, but then she opened them and saw that Helen's eyes were open, too, and the shock of seeing something so close that sees you, too, broke her up. They fell down on the bed laughing.

Ginger remembers the smell of Helen's soap in her nose, the taste of her mouth—the strange, bright wetness of another person's mouth—on her lips. They didn't kiss again, but Ginger never forgot seeing her friend's eye as big as the moon, no longer an organ of sight but a presence of its own, vast and impersonal. She felt now that she had a terrible secret from Helen, and didn't even know what it was; but it was real, as real as Grandpa Ford's face at the dinner table, his eyes screwed down tight, the kiss of death on his lips, and him way down inside, out of sight, where no one could follow.

≈

Helen's dad, full of spaghetti and meat sauce, lasts through the seventh inning. Helen covers him and whispers, "Goodnight, Daddy." No answer—he's outta there. That's it, then: grow up, fall asleep. Helen's hair hangs straight down when she tucks him in. She's just ironed it, and it shines.

The girls have changed. They're wearing kick-pleat skirts, blouses and sweaters, and black flats. In front of the hall mirror Ginger smoothes Autumn Frost onto her lips and blots it. They look back at themselves from the mirror. It's a nice moment, serious: Two girls whose only wish is to get inside a radio station, be where the music is. What can be so hard? If those girls in New York can get into the Beatles' hotel room, they figure they can get inside their very own WBVA.

≈

Ginger and Helen crest a hill and lean back to coast down the far side, and there it is: there are two pairs of red lights on it, halfway up and at the top, and these pulse slowly to warn off airplanes. Helen's ahead, her hair flowing. She has her earphone in and swings her head from side to side, pedals furiously, then coasts, spreading her arms as if she would gather in everything: the night, the invisible waves rushing through it, and the beacon that draws them silently toward itself.

This part of town is not too familiar to them. The station, a white, single-story rectangle, sits high above the road. The girls walk their bikes up the long driveway, looking at the now-immense tower and at the houses on either side of the station. In the gloom, Ginger can see the two skinny ladders that run upward from about fifteen feet off the ground, one on either side of the tower, each one ending high up at the level of the lower lights. She stops and leans back to take it all in. She says, "Let's go up to the tower. Let's climb it."

Helen pushes a sheet of hair out of her face. "You want to get electrocuted, right?"

"It's not electric," Ginger says, but she's not positive. Things you can't see can kill you; this she knows. "It works on waves."

"*You* work on waves," Helen replies.

They dump their bikes in the long grass behind the station parking lot and walk up the hill to where the tower stands in its fenced field. Hitching up their skirts, they get over then walk around the perimeter, daring each other to test the guy wires for current. Ginger does: they're dead and cold. They lie in the grass and look up at the tower with its red lights that sizzle and dissolve and take turns using Helen's earphone. The DJ's voice, between songs, is so clear it's as if he's standing right beside them—which, in a sense, he is. But they don't recognize the voice.

The only DJ they've ever met is Bob Lewis. He was doing a remote broadcast from the shopping center. They had imagined this beautiful guy, slim, with blond hair curling around the headphones. But there he was, sitting at a card table under the awning at the ShopWell, headphones scrunched down over a dirty Orioles cap, that great voice rolling out of this *fat* body. Bob Lewis *comin' atcha.* The girls hung around for a while, drank Cokes, and accepted free WBVA sun visors from the ShopWell lady, but didn't wear them. After watching the flesh-and-blood Bob Lewis sweat for an hour, they were too embarrassed to endorse the store.

Ginger's thinking of Grandpa Ford as she starts to climb the tower. In her mind, she is climbing his tower, too, in California, back in the forties, way up on a hard bluff overlooking the ocean. Sailors can see the flicker of the red lights from their ships. She can hear the waves crashing on the rocks and the surge, like deep breathing, as the wave is sucked back into the sea. It's quiet in the studio. The dark, cool rooms are lined with shelves of records heavy as dinner plates. Grandpa Ford leans forward in his chair; his lips are an inch from the microphone. He's going to a commercial, and he'll be right back.

This is rough going. Ginger shinnies up a diagonal beam, gets her feet onto a crossbeam, and looks around. Helen's a shadow a couple of stories away. Ginger looks down on the flat roof of the radio station, its pools of water moving in the breeze like twitching sheets, and at the toy traffic going back and forth on the road down in front.

She holds onto the cold steel and looks up. The lower light's still pretty far above her, seated in its black steel dish. When the light flares up, she sees bits of weeds sticking out from beneath the dish, and in another flash she sees a bird tumble out of the nest and fly off.

It's getting dark fast. Ginger edges over to the ladder and kicks off her shoes, which pitter-patter down through the shell of emptiness. Helen yells something she can't make out, but that doesn't matter: what she's really saying is that she's *not kidding*.

Ginger's halfway up the ladder when she stops to rest, not because she's tired, not exactly; but her legs won't go. So she folds her arms around the ladder and lays her cheek against the cold rung. She imagines Grandpa Ford at the Grand Canyon. She is standing beside him, they grip the railing and grin at each other, and then they look out into magnificence.

Ginger decides to go all the way to the top.

She crawls up the ladder, but as she reaches the top rung, the signal to her legs fails and they sag forward against the ladder rungs. A flutter runs through them, and a faintness flushes upward into the hollow of her belly. She holds tightly to the ladder and closes her eyes. Helen is talking again: she's *real* excited. "Shut up, just shut up," Ginger says, but her voice is so small she knows Helen can't hear it. Her kneecaps are fusing to the steel and a giddy, sick feeling is passing in waves through her legs, which seem to float like empty clothes.

Ginger's hands are like clamps on the ladder, but when she looks at them they seem to conceal a malevolent life, and in terror that they will spring open she shuts her eyes again. She sees them crossed over her chest, bleached white, the fingernails framing little dead half-moons. The headline GIRL FALLS INTO THIN AIR, DIES floats across her vision. "Stop, now," she says. "Please." But it won't stop.

The room is shadowy and still, candle-flickering, but people are weeping. They come over to look at her and weep, even the men, and she knows she mustn't open her eyes. Helen's dad is there, alert and sorry. Her own parents are there, but unseen. Grandpa Ford comes over. He's wearing his blue blazer with the silver buttons. He's alive, he looks healthy, never better. "Son of a bitch," she says. "You bastard." He opens his mouth in a wide smile and Ginger sees that his teeth are black and that's when she screams. She can't tell if she's falling, but the whirling inside her opens out and out and everything inside her rips away and vanishes. Her voice whips out of her and flies away over the canyon. She sees a huge, glittering still thing and focuses on it: it's the eye of a bird, and even though she tries, she can't fall into it. It's beautiful, but it's not hers. She puts her mouth over the rung in front of her face and bites down until the pain—a pain she thought until now was only for him—stops her.

≈

After a while she hears a voice and feels a vibration in the tower. Someone's coming up.

"Hold on," a voice says—a man's voice. "Just stay there, hold on," he says, and she wants to laugh. It's Bob Lewis's voice. Bob Lewis is comin' at her.

≈

After Bob talks her down—smooth guy—she stumbles, nearly falling, marveling, into Helen's arms. Helen's crying, then Ginger cries. Two girls having a good cry. Bob is sprawled on the ground. This is not a guy who climbs towers very often. "This is a dangerous thing," he says, placing a hand on his belly and breathing hard. "A dangerous thing you're doing."

He says he's late, that they'd better come inside, and they agree—after all, that's what they came for. He takes them down the hill and into the station. In the studio, the other DJ's already putting on his jacket. He hardly looks at the girls. He and Bob talk for a minute while "Green Onions" plays, and after the other guy leaves, Bob cues another record and pours himself a cup of coffee. He motions for them to sit down and puts a finger to his lips: they're in the studio and *on the air*.

Ginger closes her eyes and the music plays. Bob plays all their favorites. Once, when he goes out to check the teletype machine, she goes up to the microphone. She doesn't even know if it's switched on, but she wants to do something. Helen's waving at her to stop, but she can't help it: She leans over and speaks—just a whisper— into the microphone. This isn't his kind of music, so who knows if he's even listening? But if he is, she wants him to know—she wants the anonymous world to know—that she's here.

Next morning, Ginger wakes up early, gets dressed, leaves Helen sleeping, and lets herself out. The air is cool, and it's quiet; nothing to hear but the sound of her bicycle tires swishing over the pavement. Everyone's still in bed when she gets home, and she walks quietly through the house and up the stairs. She taps on Grandpa's door with a fingernail and when there's no answer, she pushes the door open. His room's dark. She keeps her eyes open, waiting for whatever light there is to fill them.

Grandpa Ford's under the blankets, curled up like a fiddlehead. His mouth is open and he's drooled a little. Ginger holds her breath, waiting for a movement or a sound of breathing. She puts her hand over his hand and his fingers tighten around the radio he's holding. She traces the braided cord to his ear and gently takes out the earphone. Listen: It's a voice out of the past, unhurried and mellow, saying that there will be a brief announcement, and a pause, and then the news. We'll be right back. Stay right there.

When she pulls the curtains, Grandpa stirs and moans. The sun pours its light into the room. Ginger raises the sash and right on cue some birds begin to call. She leans out the window and spots them: some are in the trees, others are walking over the grass. She leans out farther to wave, and this breaks up the party. Some of the birds fly off. Others drop down onto the grass, alert, startled, and cock their heads at her in a moment of wonder.

The End Zone

My folks are dead. They died a year ago this March, when their car went off the bridge between here and the town of Clay, which is where I go to school. The Fairlin River, in whose waters they drowned, is a culvert running down out of the Appalachians, dirty as hell from the pollution the Clay mills pour into it, and it boils, swelling up as gray and ugly as any other river in these hills when the snow melts early in the spring. That's when it got them.

They were on their way to see Dad's sister, Ruth, and they broke through just beyond midpoint of the bridge. Dad's Ford plowed through the guard rails, tipped over, back to front, and landed on its top. They found it lying on the bottom like that, snugged up against one of the cement pilings. It was raining; it was night. They hadn't much chance of getting out, and they died. The sheriff said that it was probably a quick death, but how he arrived at this conclusion, I don't know—and don't want to know.

My sister, Ellie, and I went with our dad's brother, Frank—we live with him and his wife, Alice, now—to the scene of the departure the following day. It looked like a tank had gone through there. Ellie wouldn't get out of the car, but I went and looked over. I had expected this to be horrible, that I would find myself standing face to face with what had killed them, but holding onto the railing and leaning out, all I could see was the river, and since it had cleared of silt overnight, the frame of Dad's car with its muffler and tailpipe swaying loosely in the current.

There was a long time after that, months, that I wouldn't travel in a car: walked everywhere—to school, to track practice, home again.

No one seemed to think this odd. I'd wash and wax Alice's station wagon, but that was just for the fun of it. Or I'd sit on the hood after supper and lay back on the windshield and listen to the radio, watching as the windows flashed to yellow one by one and the sky darkened above the house—their house, of course, not Ellie's and mine.

We used to live not more than two miles from here.

One afternoon I walked out of my way to go by there on my way home, and the old house was sitting there just as ordinary as you please. For a weird moment I imagined walking up the sidewalk and going inside—I could see the screen door was still disfigured from where Ellie and I pushed on it in our haste to get out of the house one day a long time ago when Mom was after us, to spank us for something. We were laughing—Ellie was screaming with laughter and crying, too, and I was trying to get the door unfastened. Mom did catch up with us, and she did spank us. It wasn't so bad. By the time Dad got home we were all friends again. I don't think anyone even mentioned it. It was just—a day.

I took a long look at that pushed-out screen door, and then I walked on. I didn't go by there again.

≈

I sloshed the wet snow off the windshield of Alice's car and watched Uncle Frank pull into the driveway too fast, slewing the van's rear end around. The driveway's on a grade—mostly red mud, this time of year, but studded between the ruts with a backbone of clean rocks. Frank revved the engine as he put the van into second gear and brought it, coughing and trembling, up to the house.

Frank and Alice never had any children and getting us this way didn't exactly make their lives complete. I don't know whether Alice couldn't have children or whether they just didn't want any, but they had little choice, I believe, where Ellie and I were concerned: Aunt Ruth couldn't afford us, even with the money from the estate—a few dollars on the house, some savings—so it was live with Frank and Alice or go to a foster home.

I wanted to go and live with my friend, Bill, but Alice said no, we would stay with the family, both of us: how could I even *think* of going to live with *strangers*? I guess it didn't occur to her that, at the time, she seemed like the stranger.

About a week after Ellie and I had been living there, Ellie knocked one of Alice's porcelain figurines onto the floor and broke it. There was so much of the stuff around you could hardly avoid running into it, and Ellie's pretty clumsy, besides. Alice rushed in from the kitchen, saying, "Oh, oh, oh," and gathered up the pieces. Ellie offered to glue it (I can just picture that) but Alice just ran to her bedroom and shut the door. Frank finally coaxed her out, and by the time we sat down to dinner, she was as self-possessed as ever, which is to say, about as pale and brittle as one of her porcelain people.

And Frank. Frank was nice enough, but he had a habit of slipping into your peripheral vision just before disappearing; one minute he'd be there, the next, you'd hear him out in his shop, working on some project. Not that he wasn't good—cabinetmaking was his line—but he took on a lot of extra work and was at it nights and weekends after Ellie and I came; and on our account, I guess.

We were all fairly unhappy. We spent a lot of time trying not to break anything.

But Bill was no stranger, not to me. We were best friends, had been since the first grade. Bill was overweight by around fifty pounds but quick, real energetic and outgoing. We were on the track team together, which is what you might do at Clay High if you were a guy and couldn't play a team sport. Bill threw the shot, and I ran, mainly the 220 dash, sometimes the relays. When we could get dates—which wasn't often—we doubled in Bill's dad's car, a big Chrysler.

Bill loved to drive, eat, and talk about God. Bill fought what he called "chronic" bad breath by sucking on mints whenever he wasn't actually eating something more substantial. I once suggested to him that too many sugary mints could cause bad breath, but he shook his head—he needed a broader context; his breath, he said, was an *affliction*.

"It's destroying me socially, man. That's why Ellie won't go out with me."

I could hear the mints clicking against his back teeth.

"She can't get around the old buffalo breath," he said.

But the real reason Ellie wouldn't go out with Bill was that I told her, if she did, I would kill her. Friendship is one thing, but she is my sister. I didn't want Bill snuggling up to Ellie in the back seat of that big car to talk about God, or any of his afflictions.

≈

Frank opened the back doors of the van and began to unload some chairs he'd brought home for stripping. He put the chairs in the shop and came over to the car and leaned in at my window, the sharp, woody smells of pine pitch and bourbon drifting in with the snow.

I knew he drank—and drank on the job now and then. There was a pint bottle in the tool box.

"That road's a damn mess," he said. "Don't you go and land Alice's car in a ditch. Where're you heading?"

"Down to Somer's to get some new boots."

I had fifty dollars of trust money in my pocket, the last of my Christmas allowance.

"Are you covered?" Frank's hand strayed to his pants pocket and hovered there, like maybe he was about to pull a fast draw.

But here was something. He was going to pretend to offer me money he didn't really have and I was going to pretend to refuse it, even though I knew it probably didn't exist in the first place.

"I'm covered," I said.

Frank grinned. He put his face up into the light snow and, to my surprise, stuck out his tongue to catch some flakes.

"Well, drive careful. I better get on in the house. I'm beginning to feel like a damn popsicle."

≈

Somer's is a factory store and every shoe in the place is defective— crooked seams and such—and you wait on yourself. It's like you work there.

I found the boots I wanted and tried one of them on. It felt great. I walked over to the foot mirror to check the before-and-after look, the new standing next to the old, then boxed the boots and laced up my old one. The boots were on sale for $49.95 but when I laid my fifty dollars down the clerk hesitated, then looked at me and smiled: I had forgotten about the tax. But he let me write my name and telephone number on the register slip and told me to bring the money in sometime.

Outside, the snow had thinned almost to nothing and some sky was showing in the west. Track practice would begin in a week; the first meet was less than a month away. I would be up for the 220 and the 440, but nothing longer. I tried the mile once, last year, because Coach told me I had the form for it, but I finished just about dead last.

David Walker was worse than me, although that's not saying much. Walker couldn't be talked out of losing. He'd start out like everybody else, but by the time he'd been lapped by all the other runners, he would have settled into his true pace: a painful lurch toward a full-length touchdown in the cinders. A couple of us would scoop him up and walk him around so he wouldn't cramp too badly. When he could breathe again, he'd clean his glasses on his shorts, check out whatever skin damage he'd taken, and head for the showers. This happened at nearly every meet and came to be seen, to Coach's embarrassment, as an event in itself.

I took my box of boots through the kitchen door. Alice was sitting at the kitchen table drinking a cup of coffee.

"What do you have there, Phil?" Alice asked me without looking up.

"New boots." I put the box on the table and opened it. The smell of fresh leather rose over the table.

"Ooh," she said, musically, and flipped back the tissue paper with a finger. She looked into the box and I had the feeling she was assessing more than just the cost of footwear. Alice settled her gaze on her cup again.

"How much did those set you back?"

"Fifty dollars." I didn't tell her about the tax because I could see that she was mad at either Frank or Ellie and would very shortly be letting me have some of it, if I hung around. I picked up the box and made for the stairs.

"Dinner's in exactly half an hour," Alice said.

Up in my room, I sat on the bed and laced up the boots. The left boot felt fine but the other—the one I hadn't tried on in Somer's—was too tight. Way too tight. I re-tied it, loosely, giving it extra room across the top, but it was still too tight. I compared the soles and checked the size numbers printed inside the boots: everything matched. I walked around the room and did some deep knee bends, trying to stretch the leather.

My foot was hurting, now. I walked around the room three times and with every other step I felt an evil pinch to my right foot.

I took the boots off, crushed them into the tissue paper, and threw the box into the closet.

I woke up early enough the following morning, Saturday, to get breakfast while it was still hot. Alice had said, "I'm not a waitress and this isn't a hotel," and she wasn't kidding. I was halfway dressed when I remembered the boots. I took the box out of the closet and dumped them onto the bed, where they jumped once and then lay still, the glossy waffle soles gleaming like big shiny teeth in a big smile. I decided to try them again in the light of a new day.

I minced down the stairs and into the kitchen. Ellie was sitting at the table in her bathrobe. She looked sweet, I have to admit. Alice was at the stove. Frank stood at the open door, drinking coffee. The room was warm and was spiced with the smell of bacon and Bisquick pancakes. My right foot was throbbing.

"Morning, Doodlebug," I said to Ellie—just for fun.

She gave me her bored look; then she glanced down. "*Work* boots," she said. "How utterly fascinating."

Alice turned and eyed the boots. "Those are very nice, Phil," she said.

"Nice if you're a farmer," Ellie said.

"El-lie," Frank growled. "Be nice."

"I am a farmer, and so are you, Doodlebug. We come from a long line of farmers."

Ellie sighed and took a sip of juice. "Why do you keep calling me that? It's so sickening."

Alice said, "There are no farmers in this family, Phil."

"Well—hicks, then."

Alice turned from the stove, wiping her hands on her apron. "That is a word I don't like to hear. Do you want two eggs or three?"

"Give him three," Ellie said. "He's a chicken farmer." She grinned at me.

Frank said, "Doodlebug. I knew a fellow once who was called that."

Ellie screamed with laughter. I began to flap my hands and cluck. I dived under the table and pecked, so to speak, at Ellie's bare feet. She laughed and kicked; then she pulled back and gave me a good one square on the ear.

"Jesus *Lord*," I said. "That really hurt, Ellie."

"Well, you shouldn't go after people's feet." Then she saw the look on my face. Flushing, she said, "I'm sorry. I didn't think it was that hard."

"Forget it," I said. I eased into a chair to take the weight off my foot. They were all looking at me.

"Phil, what is it?" Alice asked.

"One of these goddamned boots doesn't fit," I said. "And I can't take them back because they were on sale."

"I don't understand," Alice said. "You bought boots that don't fit?"

"Just one of them," I said. "The other one fits fine."

"Well, hell," Frank said. He edged a little ways out the door.

"Dumb hick farmer," Ellie said.

"Be *quiet*, Ellie." Alice threw eggshells in the garbage can and looked at Frank, then at me. "Did you even try them on in the store?"

I pulled off the boot that had caused the trouble and held it up.

"This is the one I didn't try on. I did try on the other one and for some reason, I guess I wasn't thinking, I figured they'd fit the same, just like always. I've never noticed that one of my feet is bigger than the other. Never even thought about it. Do you ever think about stuff like that, Frank? That you might not match the way you always thought you would?"

"Hey, hey," Frank said. "Settle down, now."

Ellie said, "Phil, it doesn't matter"—but I wished she had come out with something smart.

"Of course it matters," I said.

"Fifty dollars," Alice said quietly. "Phil, we just don't have that kind of money to throw away."

"It was my goddamned money."

"Hey!" Frank said. He made a cop's slow-down signal with his hands, then jammed his hands in his pockets. He looked miserable.

"I'm going over to Bill's," I said.

"Can I come?" Ellie asked.

Alice was smiling but her face was sad and hard. She did a slow turn back to the stove. Frank, outside now, said, "They look like good boots. What size are they?"

Alice began to cry.

I looked across the table at my sister but I couldn't speak—her face at that moment looked so much like Mother's, I wished that I had drowned, too, that we had all gone down together in the car that night; wished that I would never again have to sit in a strange room and see the pain on my sister's face and not be able to do anything about it.

I grew dizzy suddenly. I realized I had been holding my breath. When I filled my lungs the room seemed to slant and a handful of black sparks shimmered across my field of vision. Ellie and Alice seemed to be sliding away from me, going over an invisible edge, and I would be the next to go if I didn't get out.

I ran upstairs and got into my old boots, then skirted the kitchen and went out the front door.

Frank's keys were in the van. Ellie came out and ran across the yard. She stood in the mud in her bare feet and banged on the window.

"Let me come," she shouted.

"Go back inside."

"Let me come with you. *Please*, Phil."

"No."

≈

Bill's mom answered the door. She was wearing a floaty pink house-dress with sleeves that ended in two explosions of blue fluff. She lifted one of these and aimed it toward the rear of the house. "I wouldn't say for sure," she said. "But I believe Sir Laurence is in the rehearsal hall."

I heard Bill muttering behind the door—then a shout. Our class was putting on Macbeth and Bill was playing Macduff. He was lying on the bed, holding his script at arm's length, when I came in. He smiled a big stagey smile.

"My ever-gentle cousin, welcome hither," he said.

"Let's go for a ride. I've got the van."

"It's early, isn't it? I'm running my lines." After a pause, he said, "What's up?"

"Nothing. Hey—I think there's some whiskey in the truck."

"All right!" Bill leaped up, then crumpled back onto the bed. He pressed the script to his belly. "All my pretty chickens?" he moaned.

"You want to give it a rest?"

"You're touchy. Don't you like art?"

"I love it."

Bill pulled a fresh shirt from the closet and put it on. There were shirts lying all over the room. "Exeunt," he said.

Bill's mom met us at the front door. "I wouldn't ask," she said. "But where are you going?"

"Out," Bill replied. "We're going to drink whiskey and roll the van and die tragically on the highway."

"Fine," she said. "Just be back here by suppertime."

"Okay, Mom."

"Fine," she said, and floated back down the hall.

～

We could see the school's brick bell tower from the bridge. "The school, the old school, and nothing but the school," Bill sang out. The sun had soaked into a gray sky; snow was beginning to fall again. I parked the van and we walked to the football field, passing Frank's pint bottle of bourbon back and forth. We ate some snow to kill the taste.

I saw a movement across the field and quickly stuck the bottle into my back pocket.

"What? Who is that?" Bill said.

Whoever it was, was running, not toward us, but along the bleachers on the other side of the field. When he reached the end zone he tapped the goalpost, turning, and ran down along our side.

"Jesus Lord," Bill said. "It's Walker."

David Walker saw us when he was still about twenty yards away. He slowed down then and jogged over to us.

"Oh, hi," he said. "It's you guys. What're you doing here?"

"What're *you* doing here?" Bill replied—clever boy. He grinned, elbowing me as Walker took off his fogged glasses and wiped them clean with the waistband of his sweatsuit.

"Getting in shape," Walker said.

"We were just out," I said.

"Out and about. Just having a few little drinks," Bill said. "You look like you could use one. Want a drink?"

Walker put on his glasses and took us in one at a time with his owl's eyes. "No. No, I guess not. Thanks."

"Hell of a day," I said. I wanted to move this conversation along.

Walker looked out over the field. The snow had picked up and was slanting across it in a stinging wind.

"I guess it is," he said. "The season's almost here. Well, I better get back to it."

Bill had wandered downfield and was reciting Shakespeare into the wind, throwing his arms for effect. Walker and I watched him for a minute and then Walker said, "You guys really drinking?"

I shrugged. "Just enough to keep out the cold."

Walker looked at me—a disapproving, sophomore look; then he glanced at the whitening field.

"Come on, I'll race you once around. If you're not too drunk."

I recalled Walker pitching over finish lines at home and away, sobbing for breath. "Okay," I said.

We walked over to where the sidelines should have shown and got lined up, shoulder to shoulder.

"Go," Walker whispered.

I left the crouch too fast, took one stride, and fell. Walker was already twenty feet ahead of me. I got up and ran hard, trying to catch up. The wind was at our backs and I settled into a steady run: I would let him pace me until we were halfway around, then I would take him.

I caught up near the end zone and swung inside, slowing down to take the corner. Then I saw that Walker was wearing spikes; he didn't slip an inch. Coming out of the corner I fell again and scrambled up and ran on as fast as I could. By this time he was far ahead. I put on all the speed I had.

I heard Bill yelling hoarsely from the middle of the field as Walker pounded on ahead of me, really moving. The distance between us hadn't closed. I saw him turn at the far end of the field. His arms were dropping. He reached out to touch the leg of the goalpost with his fingertips as he went by it.

I put my head down and forced myself to move a little faster, and by the time I reached the goalpost I couldn't negotiate the turn and fell again, heavily, into the end zone. This time I didn't get up.

I rolled onto my back and closed my eyes. Snowflakes pattered onto my face and into my mouth as I pulled in the air. When I opened my eyes the sky swirled and then everything out there irised in a tight quarter-turn and stopped dead. Walker's head swam into view.

"Get up," he panted. "Sprint to the finish."

Walker stood over me, clutching his knees, blowing steam into my face. I was hot in the middle and cold at the edges and my stomach was knotted around the sour booze.

"Can't," I said. "You go ahead without me."

"Cute," Walker said. "That's really funny."

I heard squishy footsteps. "God, man, are you okay?" Bill said.

"He's all right," Walker said. He turned back to me. His fogged lenses were beautiful, cloudy opals. "He's just out of shape. Get up." He grabbed my arm. "Come on, *get up*."

I pulled away from him and rolled to my knees.

"Keep your Goddamned hands off me," I said. "I'm telling you, Walker, don't touch me again."

"You said you'd race."

"Well, I won't. I'm finished. Congratulations."

"You said you'd race," he persisted.

"Hey! Are you deaf, or what?" Bill shouted. "He just said—"

"Shut up, Bill," I said.

By now I was thoroughly chilled, my guts burned, and I was shaking all over. I scooped up two handfuls of snow and clenched my fists until the stuff compacted, burning me like iced steel. I closed my eyes.

I saw myself reaching out with long arms as Dad's car groaned through the rupture it had made, saw the burst railing hanging like broken strings and the car hesitating on the brink, felt a snake twist through me as the car up-ended and all sound, just before the moment of impact, was sucked, like their last breaths, from the sky.

I scooped up more snow and rubbed my face with it. I couldn't breathe. Streams of icy water ran down into my collar and over my chest. I was already cold. Now I would be completely cold.

Walker whipped off his glasses. Without them he looked dazed; his glare was skewed. "Stop it," he said.

But I didn't want to stop. I moved my fingers by manipulating the cold wires running through them, bringing the snow to my mouth and swallowing the lump before it had time to melt.

Walker got down on his knees and grabbed my shoulders. "Stop this and get up," he said. "Get up and race."

I threw off his hands and screamed in his face. "*You son of a bitch. My parents are dead.*"

He looked at me with bare, stony, terrible eyes.

"You lose, then," he said softly.

I lunged, knocking Walker over, then climbed on top of him and punched him in the face. It felt good. I settled in to punch him some more but he twisted, braced himself, and abruptly sat up—I got the top of his head square on the mouth. I covered my lips, pressing hard to contain the pain in my mouth while Walker pounded and pushed me. I grabbed at his flailing arms and found his hands. We stayed like that for a moment: me sitting on him, our hands clasped, neither of us moving. Blood was dripping off my chin. My eyes were so dazzled with tears that I couldn't see anything except a glare of blue; then, faintly, the tall uprights of the goalposts floated up out of the watery weather and into my view.

I felt hands slide under my arms and I let go of Walker, was pulled backward, lifted, and Bill laid me out on the field.

⁓

"Now that that's over, I could sure use a drink," Bill said.

"I dropped the bottle." I got up slowly and looked around at the world: bleachers, sky filled with cold sparks, blear of snow over the ground. Walker was stamping his feet and wiping his face, putting himself together. He was bloody, too.

"Some terrific race," Bill said.

"Will you for sweet Jesus' sake shut up," I said.

"What did I say?" Bill said. He turned to Walker. "What did I say?"

"Not over yet," Walker said to me. He put on his glasses. "Fifty yards to go."

"You're nuts," Bill said. "*Both* of you. Banana bread with nuts."

Walker and I hunkered down together. He looked over and grinned, his eyes slanty behind the smeared lenses. "Run like hell," he advised me.

We hit the fifty-yard line at about the same time, finishing the race roughly where we had started, but neither of us stopped there. We kept running, made the turn at the goalpost and headed downfield. Walker got ahead of me and pretty soon he was swallowed up in the snow. Putting on speed, he lifted his arms and in a moment had faded like a ghost into the whiteness of the end zone.

I didn't make the turn. I ran straight off the field and into the parking lot, passing the empty school building. I heard Bill yelling my name. I ran down the empty street, hearing my shoe-slaps echo off the storefronts, then on past the entrance to the mill. It was all downhill from here. I was running like hell. Over the roofs of the houses I could see the line of trees that twisted through the valley along either side of the river.

The bridge was the old steel trestle type with a steel mesh deck, painted black except for a shiny section of new railing in the middle of the span. As I crossed the railroad tracks that ran at a right angle to the bridge, I slouched to a walk, put my arms around myself, and listened to the sound of blood surging through my ears.

I was still a little ways off—but I could make out someone leaning against the unpainted aluminum railing, a young woman in a blue coat. As I moved closer she lifted her head out of her arms and my heart began to thump again.

It was Ellie.

She looked my way as I stepped onto the bridge. The steel trembled from the punishment its foundations were taking, and as Ellie and I walked toward each other across the emptiness above the open water I felt the river's vibration run up through the soles of my feet and into my bones, as if some spirit of steel and water—of blood and bone—were shaking me.

"I was just remembering something," Ellie said. I could hardly hear her for the drumming of the water and leaned over to listen.

"Pooky," Ellie said. "Mom used to call me that. Do you remember? She had this little song about me. She sang that I had pooky eyes, that I was her little pooky girl. Do you remember that, Phil?"

I nodded even though I did not remember.

"Pooky," she said again. "I have no idea what that means." She looked at me, then frowned and put her fingers on my lips. "You'll be in trouble," she said. "You've been in a fight."

I took Ellie's hands and we stood for a long time looking down into the noisy chasm where our parents had gone.

Bill came by a little later with the van. I wrapped Ellie up in some furniture blankets Frank kept in the back, then threw one around my own shoulders and drove Bill home. It was a quiet ride, and with him in the van, that's saying something.

At home, Alice asked few questions, but only a few. She hustled Ellie down the hall and put her into a hot bath. I needed one, too, and while I waited my turn I made a pot of coffee. When it was ready, I took a cup up to my room, pulled off my wet clothes, and put on my robe. I dug through the stuff in my closet until I found my track shoes. There were still tufts of dried grass from last season stuck on some of the spikes.

I heard the sound of the van's rear doors opening and went to the window. Frank was down in the driveway, going through the tool box.

I opened the window. "Hey, Frank," I called. "I like your boots."

He was wearing my new boots.

"I took the whiskey, Frank," I said.

Frank looked up at me with a face that was almost a pure blank.

"They fit pretty good," he said—but quietly. "How much do you want for them?"

"Fifty dollars," I said. "I'll give you a break on the tax."

He looked relieved. "Sold," he said.

I shut the window.

In the *Prairie Schooner* Book Prize in Fiction series

Last Call: Stories
By K. L. Cook

Carrying the Torch: Stories
By Brock Clarke

Nocturnal America
By John Keeble

The Alice Stories
By Jesse Lee Kercheval

*Our Lady of the Artichokes and
Other Portuguese-American Stories*
By Katherine Vaz

Call Me Ahab: A Short Story Collection
By Anne Finger

Bliss and Other Short Stories
By Ted Gilley

To order or obtain more information on these
or other University of Nebraska Press titles,
visit www.nebraskapress.unl.edu.